THE CROP CIRCLE

Kevin Sweeney

Black Rainbows Press

For Mooresboy and Higg
"Be still, quilt-child, for all is well in the world."

THE SHORT, sharp blade split open the tough skin of the scrotum and fingers clad in rubber forced their way into the opening to hook out the testicles.

They were like blind eyes, the sight organs of some creature that had evolved in a cave, millions of years atrophying them.

A pair of scissors cut the tubes which could have been optic nerves.

"A fuck-off massive cock with a pair of fuck-off massive fucking bollocks…"

A change of air pressure as a door was opened didn't entirely arouse Robin from the hypnagogic nonsense of half-sleep in which these words and images floated; instead it was the sound of chair legs scraping as the woman made herself comfortable.

Robin blundered up from the codeine induced doze.

The drugs kept the worst of pain at bay.

Robin had been sketching before dozing, finishing the last story arc of "The Transition of Mary-Sue Everyman", *the final few issues of* GENDER WARS. *Really, with the drugs making everything pleasantly fuzzy it wasn't the best time to be doing so, but Robin was eager to finish before the very end.*

And it helped to keep from brooding about the boys.

The deaths.

Robin had nodded into half-sleep, the sketches unfinished when the visitor had knocked on the partially open door. She was wearing cotton gloves and so the effort was merely theatre. Her nearly silent knock was only a prelude to letting herself in, and carefully closing the door behind her.

Scraping the chair legs across the wooden floor was a deliberate act to rouse the nodding patient.

"Good afternoon, Robin" she said, but not looking at the patient in the bed; her gaze darted here and there, taking in the bright and cheerful yet oddly bland decor of the room. "Forgive me for addressing you by your given Christian name, but... well, to be honest, normally I don't speak to my targets at all."

She was well-spoken, her voice polished and musical, but it had some weird flaw running through it, one note that jarred. Robin was always a visual person, and the woman's voice painted a peculiar picture, a figure playing with wine glasses, glasses full of various amounts of water, around the rims of which the figure's fingers ran in circles to produce different tones... only one of the glasses was cracked and out of harmony with the others, and instead of a measure of water, it was full of blood.

That was her voice.

The woman herself was in her sixties. She was tall and lean and her hair was the grey of snow clouds, hanging right down to her waist. Long grey hair always made Robin think of hippies for some reason, but her powder blue trouser suit was tailored and expensive looking, and her face held a smile that did not touch her eyes. She wore no jewellery, no earrings or necklace or rings, but there was a rainbow flag pin fixed to her lapel.

She didn't have a handbag, and when she sat herself in the visitor's chair her eyes finally stopped bouncing back and forth to settle on Robin's face.

"I'm sorry?" Robin said, confused, still only half awake.

"Most people are," said the stranger. "That's why the Catholics rely on confession, getting as much of the sorry out of the way as possible, not letting it build up through life. One of my husbands was Catholic. He said it was like brushing your teeth, confession, removing the plaque of guilt that builds up, because if you let it get out of hand it'd start to rot them, and then where was your smile? Full of holes!"

Robin had no idea what was going on.

"So now, so now, down to business," said the visitor. "I'll be brief, little bird, as I hate wasting time." She folded her gloved hands in her lap. "Normally my job involves silencing people who may cause problems for my employer, but in your case maybe I won't deem it necessary if you speak plainly and elucidate for me. Murder is only a part of what I do anyway; more generally speaking,

I tie up loose ends, and you can help me with the knots. So, the circle; tell me all."

Robin was dumbfounded by this bizarre little speech.

"What are..."

The woman reached over and put a finger on her target's lips.

"I hear a question coming, ah, ah! Time is against us, little bird! I have explained precisely as much as I need to for the moment. What I need you to do is simply to tell..." she noticed the sketchpad lying on Robin's lap. She picked it up and regarded it for a moment. "You are a comic creator, writing and drawing all your own material, so you certainly have the skills to tell it to me as a story."

One eyebrow raised as she examined the sketch of Miss Ophelia Gynist, the anti-heroine of GENDER WARS.

"This lady has never had children," she murmured. "My god, those are some ferocious bosoms. My daughter is a tit girl, I bet she'd be into this."

"Tell you what as a story?" Robin asked, bewildered. Was it the drugs? Were the painkillers not only muffling the pain, but turning what was possibly an entirely sensible exchange between them into vague nonsense?

The woman looked up from the sketch, her smile jumping back into place.

"The circle," she said.

"What circle?" Robin asked.

The smile dropped a fraction. Just behind it was a face that said; Do Not Fuck With Me.

"I suppose the drugs are making you a bit stupid," she said eventually. "How do I put this? Hmm. Ah... your friends. You know about them?"

Robin said nothing.

"The police came and spoke to you about them. The deaths were bad, but were they connected? One after another, all in the space of a week, one, two, three! The police came and spoke to you because of your bond, best chums since childhood."

Two weeks before, yes, they had. They wouldn't tell more than the absolute minimum, and Robin had been too stunned by the news that Dildo and Fat Andy and Shades had each... well, the exact details hadn't been revealed.

Only the body count.

"But you were unable to throw any light upon the matter. You don't know why each did what they did."

It was just something else to lie here and wonder about, as Robin had done for a fortnight. What HAD they each done? Beyond murder, which apparently had no discernible motive -the whole reason the officers had visited, to discern the "why" if they could- Robin didn't know what had happened.

And apart from the horror that the boys had each done something monstrous in the world, there was something else as well, wasn't there? It was deep under the layers of disbelief and confusion, this news coming as it did, when it did, but yes, buried deeply under everything was... relief.

Relief that they would never see Robin this way.

Like mum, the last time she had come to visit, finally fleeing with tears in her eyes, unable to believe what was happening to her only child...

The woman was speaking again, her bright amber eyes fixed and glittering.

"A little over a month ago you and your friends visited a field of winter wheat and made a crop circle. That is the story I wish to hear. Tell it to me and... and I am feeling generous. I'll tell you what we have established, all the whats and wherefores... and even the why."

"What do you mean?" Robin asked.

"Just what I say. I'm here to tie up a loose end; the report on what happened isn't complete without your testimony. This is strictly a form filling exercise. My employers are exceptionally thorough, as am I."

"You know what happened to the boys? To my friends?"

"Say now, say now, I do believe it's getting through!" crowed the visitor in her flawed sing-song voice. "Yes, and it is intimately tied in with the crop circle you four made. As I said, I have a report that needs rounding out, and what I need to round it out with is your testimony... why and how you four fools did what you did."

Robin's brain was fumbling towards an understanding of the bizarre situation.

This strange woman knew something, maybe everything, about what had happened to the boys, what they had each done and why they had done it, whatever terrible atrocities, though what it could possibly have to do with the circle... but, again, she claimed to be able to shed light on that too.

"You know what happened to Shades, and Dildo..."

"And the chappy you called Fat Andy, yes. Not only are copies of the police investigations as they stand within my report, but I was also able to attend at the scene of the final... hmmm, well I suppose the word would be atrocity. Yes, three atrocities, each nastier than the last. The press could never reveal the full details of course, and as for speculation on why, well! Unfortunately for the greater mass of humanity, the why will never be public knowledge."

She paused, significantly.

Robin filled in the blank.

"You know why? You'd tell me?"

"Absotively posolutely!" she giggled. "As my second husband liked to put it, a devil for Spoonerisms he was!"

Thinking, marshalling and culling random threads of thought. In a jar next to the bed were two freshly cut sunflowers. They were Robin's favourite flower; dad had tried to grow a record breaker every year. It was as they were preparing the soil for that year's attempt, when Robin had turned ten only the week before, that dad had had the first seizure which had been the first indication he had cancer.

God said, having a nice life? Yes? Well don't mind me popping a couple of these diseased walnut things into the left lobe of your brain...

Hmm? Why am I doing this? Haven't you ever read the book of Job? WHERE WERE YOU WHEN I MADE THE WORLD?

I should have asked Shades about that answer; mum always said never to answer a question with another question. It was rude.

"You want me to tell you about the circle? And in return you'll tell me..."

"Everything," she finished.

Robin sat quietly for a moment, composing the story, reviewing the key points and dialogue, setting the scene, writing it like a comic script.

And then began to tell it.

THE CIRCLE
Part One

"'A FUCK-OFF massive cock with a pair of fuck-off massive fucking bollocks', if I may quote your exact words, Jewboy" said Fat Andy, thumbing his glasses back up his nose. They were new frames, and they were royally pissing him off, sliding down all the time. "That was your artistic vision, right? So what do you reckon to this cunt for a canvas?"

The cunt in question was the field that was growing below the slope of the hill they were stood on.

The boys all made noises of appreciation, though the truth was none of them knew fuck all about farming. But what stood to reason was, if you wanted to make a crop circle, you needed a field of some sort of crop growing, and Andy had certainly scouted out a field with some kind of shit growing in it.

Robin turned around. No sign of the road, no sign of anything. They were stood on the highest elevation, a swollen grassy hump of the chalk that made up the gently undulating landscape. Hedges bordering a few fallow fields, a swathe of woods to the south-east that would, eventually, form a border along the motorway that had brought them part of the way here. There weren't even any electricity pylons in sight. A relatively undisturbed, sleepy corner of southern England a few miles from the city of Winchester.

They'd parked up in a lay-by and trekked for twenty minutes, with pop up tents and rucksacks full of provisions, hopping the occasional stile and ignoring the few signs they saw that had pictures of binoculars on them and the sinister admonition that *YOU ARE BEING WATCHED*.

If anyone asked, they were twitchers, keen bird enthusiasts, on the look-out for great-tits and swallows and boobies…

Fat Andy had prepared the alibi.

Of course.

"Out of sight, out of mind," said Dillon. He was shading his eyes; paired with the expensive clothes he wore and his good looks, he could have been posing as a model for a catalogue shoot. "Nobody should disturb us, unless... how often do farmers look at their fields, my old salad dodger?"

"No idea, Dildo," said Andy. "But not often I reckon. Plants don't grow very quickly, right? Bit of a waste of time to nip out here every day and be like, 'yeah, that's another two millimetres they've gone up, lovely stuff, think I'll spend the afty-noon fucking a pig...'"

"That's not kosher, Andrew," said Shades.

Andy rubbed his chin, looking at Robin.

"Right, right, bit culturally insensitive, Jewboy here isn't allowed to eat out a pig, is he?"

"I'm not sure that's the way the Koran puts it, but yes, pigs are offensive, or something."

Robin just smiled, even if Shades had to couch his digs in religious terms, always just two steps from offering salvation to them all. Still, it felt good to smile, even if he was completely shattered. His friends banter, by turns cheerfully obscene, deliberately ignorant, and wildly racist, fuelled by Andy's relentlessly foul mouth, was a kind of medicine which he needed right now.

He'd been close to bottling this trip even just this morning, bent double over the toilet, thin vomit in the bowl below him...

"...deaf cunt," said Andy in his ear.

Robin blinked in surprise.

"Sorry?" he said.

"I called you a deaf cunt," said Andy mildly. "For I asked you a question and you didn't answer, so, rather than assume you're an ignorant twat deliberately ignoring me, I chose to believe that you were hard of hearing. And a cunt."

Robin smiled again.

"I'm so sorry to have offended you, you precious snowflake! What was the question?" he asked.

Andy grinned.

"I asked you, would this do for a canvas, for the 'fuck-off massive cock with a pair of fuck-off massive fucking bollocks', you've been dreaming about?"

"Gay," sniggered Dildo.

Robin looked down at the growing stuff where their lives would soon end.

"Yeah," he said. "It'll do."

He shielded his eyes, even though it wasn't really necessary in the gentle afternoon light.

Then he frantically started patting one of Blake's huge biceps, a dramatic display of getting his attention.

"Bloody hell Shades, ain't that your mate down there?" he asked.

They all followed his line of sight.

There was a scarecrow on the far side of the field, hanging from outstretched arms. It wore ripped jeans and a gingham shirt, and its eyes were shiny, clearly visible even from a distance as the sun caught them. Glass? That must have been to make them look more life-life.

"Yeah, that's that Jesus bloke you're always banging on about," Robin continued. "Being nailed up like that is a dead giveaway."

Shades sighed at the blasphemy.

But he still grinned.

"Prick," he said.

*****

It was hard to believe from the way they spoke to one another that they were full-grown men and not foul-mouthed schoolboys. It happened whenever they got together, this degeneration of their language and social awareness, each of them a bad influence on one another, turning back the clock on all their individual personal growth into fully functioning members of society. Each was out in the world, making their way in chosen professions, or simply making ends meet. They had responsibilities, and partners. One was almost a father, and another was dying.

This last fact was why they were all on that hillside, and why the banter was more raucous, perhaps more forced than it otherwise would have been. This was probably the last time they would be together, unchained from their lives, on one final romp as the boys before one would go and the time-travelling magic of being together again as a quartet would be over.

What bliss, ignorance; believing only one of them was facing imminent extinction.

Andrew "Fat Andy" Morgan, Dillon "Dildo" Nash-Smart, Blake "Shades" Butcher, and Robin "Jewboy" Wasser, had known each other forever. They'd grown up in houses not more than three minutes' walk from one another, had gone to the same primary and secondary schools, and experienced most of the milestones of masculinity together; Dillon and Blake had even lost their virginity to the same girl on the same night, Sammy Mariner at the year ten disco. Sammy was, as Shades told Robin and Andy later, completely off her nut on some pills that were doing the rounds, and volunteered free love to anyone who would follow her into the girl's toilets in the Science block. Fat Andy had borne this news quite calmly considering the fact that the reason neither he nor Robin had been about to avail themselves of Sammy's generous offer was because he was looking after his friend as Robin puked his guts empty of cheap vodka on the edge of the football field.

Drugs, fights, victories, failures, they had shared almost everything until the age of nineteen when the future began to pull them apart, towards separate destinies.

Fat Andy had followed his stomach and entered catering, to finally end up in charge of the kitchen in their town's biggest hotel. Eschewing the settled life, his leisure time was spent travelling; a self-confessed sex tourist, he claimed to be searching for the perfect BJ, and would always report his findings back to the group in scrupulous detail.

Dildo had wanted to become a doctor, but had burnt out spectacularly in his second year, ending up under psychiatric evaluation for three months, and was now working as a veterinary assistant now, married to the practice's senior partner.

Shades had drifted into the world of dealing until he met a lass who was Born Again and turned him onto Jesus; after he cleaned himself up he got a job as a prison officer, and marvelled how he had ended up on the other side of the bars. They were expecting their first kid just before Christmas.

And Robin had been making a name for himself as a comics creator, particularly known for the title *Gender Wars*, which, beneath its superficial surface of super-powered anti-heroes kicking the shit out of each other, was a profound mediation on issues of sex and gender in the post-post-modern landscape, that had won numerous awards not just from within the industry, but outside as well, including a controversial win for best representation of non-binary people in fiction from the LGBT+ Sci-Fi & Fantasy Alliance.

The boys met up at the pub for their individual birthdays, without fail, no matter what else may have been going on in their personal or professional lives.

Dildo always got the first round in owing to the fact that he would always draw the shortest straw; his friends would not ever let him forget that, as had become obvious in their very first dick measuring contest at the age of seven, he would always have the shortest straw.

Not that Dildo minded, as he pointed out whenever they'd gone clubbing or on holiday to Ibiza together in their late teens, the females always eyed him up first.

With Dildo getting the drinks, Fat Andy clapped his hands together and regarded his companions.

"Right then, first order of business," he said, looking at Shades, "is that delectable crumpet you conned into the outdated condition of matrimony still got a bun in the oven?"

"My Jenny is five months along now, Andrew," said Shades. "Thank you so much for asking."

"Quite all right. And are you ready to be a daddy? Last time we got together I rather fancy you were fucking bricking it."

"No Andrew," said Shades. "To be honest, I don't think I am ready, but it's happening anyway. And I trust as a single man with neither dependents or notion of settling down you're going to impart some sort of wisdom on the matter?" He pretended to speak through gritted teeth, although it was obvious there was more than a hint of real feeling in what he said. "And the Lord knows that seeing as though I've simply *loved* hearing all the wisdom and horror stories from our parents and my work colleagues on the joys of bringing life into this world, that I am going to find whatever you have to say will be utterly profound and of utmost utility."

A nibble! Fat Andy winked at Robin, who couldn't help but smirk; oh, the banter was going to be good tonight.

"Not my wisdom, dear Shades, but rather that imparted by the Good Book."

Shades' eyes narrowed slightly. The narrowing suggested that Fat Andy should tread lightly.

"And what wisdom is that?"

Fat Andy cleared his throat.

"*Spare* the rod and *spoil* the child. Just give the little fucker whatever it wants, whenever it wants, and you'll be Superdaddy."

Shades opened his mouth, then he closed it again.

"Strictly speaking," he said, slowly, "that's a paraphrase of Proverbs 13-24, and I think you've gotten the wrong end of the stick..."

"Don't think so mate. Anyway, if you'd spared Jenny your rod you wouldn't need to be bricking it, would you? That's why your old mucker Andy here prefers to plumb the piehole, no danger of sprogs if all your tadpoles end up getting digested..."

There wasn't much Shades could say to that. It was a theme that Fat Andy had explored before; the fact that he preferred a blowjob over any other kind of sex, and the fact that he had once calculated that nearly half a billion of his potential children had been eaten by prostitutes in various countries.

Done with Shades, he turned his attention to the other man at the table.

"Robin me old yid, you look like shit," said Fat Andy. "You're all puffy. Did you eat a sausage roll and have a Jewllergic reaction?"

"Judaism isn't like being a coeliac, Andrew," Shades pointed out, glad Andy's guns had turned. "Apart from the possibility of spending eternity remote from the Lord because your people killed him. But he'll forgive you, if you ask; He's a good egg like that."

Fat Andy rolled his eyes but kept his peace. Though Shades had gotten all Jesussy, at least he had the sense to couch his mission to save his friends in the anti-politically correct language they all shared.

Dildo came back from the bar, grinning. Women always ignored the ring on his hand, and he loved shooting them down. He'd told Dee once that he only had eyes for her, and it was true; but he also maintained that there was nothing wrong with being vain if you had something to be vain about, and he knew he did. He looked good, he was dressed good, and by fuck, he felt good.

And it was boy's night.

"Pint, pint, half a pint, and something piss coloured with a head that I refuse to call beer," he said, setting them down.

"It's alcohol-free, that's the only difference," said Shades. When he picked up his drink, his huge hand made the pint glass look the size of a Coke can.

"I thought it was Muslimists who weren't allowed to get three sheets-faced," said Dildo.

"I'm not drinking because I'm on shift next week and the urine tests now cover alcohol, up to forty-eight hours before hand. And here, listen, Jewboy's on halves, why don't you rag on him for that?"

"I assumed he was being thrifty," said Dildo. "Well known for it, the Semitic peoples. If he dropped a penny it'd hit him in the back of the head."

Robin smiled. His friend's relentless abuse was a balm, the aura of decades long friendship an unchanging bubble of sanity he was happy to shelter in.

But he hadn't been fast enough to, a) observe that Fat Andy knew what fried shit was like because that was all he served in his gaff, b) patiently told Shades that all religion was total bollocks believed by mouth-breathers and largely preached by child molesters, and c) asked Dildo how many hamsters he'd had to pull out of gay cunt's arses this week, and had he personally given them the kiss of life?

And because he didn't immediately attack his mates after they attacked him, they realised something was wrong, got all serious, and tried to drag the truth out of him.

The bubble popped.

Time to tell a story.

Prostate cancer.

Metastasised.

Fucking riddled with it.

Months, not years.

There was an uncharacteristic silence.

Fat Andy broke it. Because of course it would be Fat Andy who would break an awkward silence.

"So you've got your sell-by date, eh?" he said. "That's fucking shit! I mean, Jesus jumped up Christ... whoops, 'scuse me Shades, I mean jeepers creepers... but, you know... fuck."

"You've always had such a wonderful way with words," said Robin, smiling gently.

"Fuck you."

"Mate," said Dildo. He paused. "Are you sure they can't do anything?"

Robin shrugged, rolling his half pint glass back and forth in his palms.

"Anything that could be done has been. I'm still on a load of meds, but it's mainly pain management now, and stuff I take to stop me being sick because of the other stuff I have to take. Vicious circle." He sighed. Then he laughed, a short sharp sound devoid of mirth. "You know what? The consultant says they're going to try me on this other kind of chemo, a sort of last roll of the dice million to one shot... and he sits there and he tells me, very gravely, that there will be side-effects..."

He ran a hand through his thick mop of crazy black curls.

"So, Andy, the puffiness you noticed is one of those side-effects. Water-weight gain. In addition to dying, I'm growing bitch tits."

His friends said nothing. The sudden bitterness in Robin's voice was so unlike him, but it was entirely justified, wasn't it?

"I've already booked a place in a hospice, the Countess Mountbatten over in Southampton. Nice place. Mum said to come home to her and Roger, but they need taking care of themselves, and I can't do that to her. It's on the bus route from their house so they can visit every day until..."

There was a long period of time in which the loudest thing in their corner of the pub was the fruit machine merrily warbling to itself.

Shades sighed.

"Robin," he said, "don't hate me for this, but I have to..."

Fat Andy moaned. Dildo closed his eyes.

"... I have to ask you to consider the Lord. He's here for you..."

Robin held a hand up.

"Shades," he said, "can I make a suggestion? I know you want to save my soul and all that, and I'll let you try, I really will, I'll listen to your whole sales pitch again... but not tonight.

Tonight, I'd just like a few beers and a few laughs with my best mates. Okay?"

Shades considered. Then he sighed.

"Fine," he said. "But I am going to save you, all of you. Jesus is also one of my mates you know."

"Then why doesn't the cheap cunt ever stand a round?" asked Fat Andy.

"He could turn water into wine!" said Shades. "For fucks sake!"

The tension broke.

They drank. There was laughter. They talked about past victories, old flames, and blow jobs, and argued over the names of characters in cartoons they only half-remembered. They blocked out the pool table and played killer. There were tears, more laughter, and tears again. At some point, the issue of bucket lists came up... and from there was resurrected an idle thought from a dull, rainy lunchtime in year nine when the only entertainment to be had was two ancient issues of *Razzle* and a copy of the *Fortean Times* which devoted a half dozen pages to photographs of that year's crop circles.

Nobody could remember who first pointed it out, but once it was said it seemed profound. Crop circles were a sort of graffiti, and yet, during all the years that the phenomena had been going on for, with circles growing in complexity into truly gob-smacking creations -snowflakes and mandalas, fractals and interlocking gears- nobody had tackled possibly the most common subject of all anonymous art.

A dick, complete with bollocks.

It was pretty much the first thing anybody learned to draw on toilet stall walls and in the margins of text books... there was even one drawn on the corner of the desk the boys were sat at, a big cheerful pair of circles with a long cylinder jutting up between them. It was done in permanent marker, and the artist had even drawn a few drops of spunk squirting out of the tip.

They all agreed that this was a situation they would correct, in the coming summer holidays. One night they'd cycle out into the countryside, find a suitable field, and draw the biggest graffiti dick the world had ever seen; or, in the exact words of a young Robin "Jewboy" Wasser, "A fuck-off massive cock with a pair of fuck-off massive fucking bollocks."

Definitely.

Except they never had.

It was an idea that got floated from time to time, normally by Robin who was the most enamoured with the scheme, and normally when they had been passing around a half bottle of ASDA's own brand vodka they had nicked... but it never happened. And the years went by and life beckoned and grew complicated and they got jobs and relationships and had personal tragedies and minor achievements and fallings out and birthday reunions...

Then tonight had happened.

And Robin had dropped his bombshell.

Then they had got drunk.

And then the crop circle idea came around again.

ROBIN HAD been talking for over half an hour, and now was tired and thirsty.

Trying to pour a glass of Lucozade, the visitor got there first, filling the glass and passing it over with small, efficient movements.

"So now, so now," she said as Robin sipped the fizzy glucose drink. "It's much as I thought. Of course I dug into your history extensively and I knew you weren't working for one of our rivals, but it is good to have it confirmed in your own words. Just a bunch of drunken idiots in high spirits."

Then she changed the subject.

"Did you see your friends in the interim period, between that night and the day you actually did it?"

Robin nodded.

"Of course, we had to plan, and practice. We did it round at Andy's because the lazy fucker never cut his lawn, and we figured the long grass..."

Robin frowned, the brain-smog of painkillers had cleared enough during the storytelling for synapses to fire just a little bit faster.

"What did you mean by 'one of our rivals'?" The visitor waved a hand dismissively, but the question was pressed; "You said you had

answers, why not start with that? Who are you, who is 'we'?"

"Right, right, yes, quid pro quo," she said. She unfolded her gloved hands, crossed her legs, and folded her hands again. "My employer is one of the largest corporate entities in the world, primarily concerned with agricultural biotech. You probably won't have heard of us, we aren't a fucking 'brand', but if you've eaten at least one meal every day of the past week, on average at least a quarter of those meals would have contained products we have some direct hand in cultivating."

Robin mulled this information over.

"When you came in, you said... you told me that you killed people. You silenced them."

"True!"

"...and you work for a company that, what, sells seed?"

"It's far more complicated than that, but in essence, yes."

"That's crazy. Why would a company like... why do you..."

"Food production is one of the most vital industries in the whole world, little bird. Humans eat food. Everyday there are more humans. We are talking about a multi-billion-dollar market which is essential for the continuation of our species, and with such sums involved it is cut-throat to say the least. There are such things as spies and moles and sleeper agents, more so than employed by most of the world's governments. And industrial espionage has always involved a certain amount of what euphemistically used to be called 'wet work'."

Robin nodded, understanding.

"And what does that have to do with me, or my friends..."

Shutting up before the question was even fully asked, because the answer was obvious.

Wasn't it?

"The field," said the visitor, "was one of ours. It contained an experimental crop. You and your chums vandalised millions in research and development."

Robin reached for a follow-up question that would turn this answer into a more complete explanation, but she changed the subject again by asking her own question.

"But to show you there are no hard feelings... do you want to know what happened to Mr Morgan?" she asked.

FAT ANDY
Meat & Two Veg

AFTER THE dinner sitting was over Andy sent his staff home early. None of them asked why, because in Andy's kitchen you didn't second guess the head chef, and that went double when, instead of telling you how much of a useless fucking joke of a cook you were, he was being all friendly and insisting he would take care of clean up himself...

(*saveloy*)

When the door had shut on the last of his staff, Andy looked around his kitchen. The equipment and work tops were filthy with smears and stains and spills, and the industrial sized sinks were crammed full of plates waiting to be rinsed off before being loaded into the giant dishwasher, but he didn't make a move to start on any of it.

(*chipolata*)

He had one more meal to prepare.

(*over the lips and*)

He locked the door.

*****

Amanda Phelps considered her position as head of hospitality at the Crest Hotel a major step down in her career within the hotelier industry, and not even a week into the job she had settled on a suitable target to take out her frustration on... the head chef.

If asked, Amanda would have been hard pressed to say exactly why that particular member of staff became the object of her loathing. He was good at his job, and ran a tight ship all together; he stuck to his budgets, was meticulous in all areas of hygiene, and was only as brutal with his staff as most head chefs were required to be, the general rule being that human resources only got involved in kitchen politics should verbal abuse turn to physical.

He was also loud, crude, and fat. These were things Amanda loathed. Good enough reason to turn her frustrated hate upon him.

Amanda had previously worked as assistant manager for a boutique spa which boasted minor royalty amongst its clientele. Then she had been... indiscreet. There had been a... temptation.

She was only human.

Really, it was all blown well out of proportion, but in the end, blood had been demanded, and it was hers that had been shed.

She was told she was lucky that the other parties involved had asked for the matter to be hushed up, and that she was twice as lucky to be getting any kind of recommendation at all, a recommendation for a position with another establishment in the parent company's portfolio... in exchange for her ongoing silence on the sordid affair.

The stress and indignity of it all had made her pile on the pounds; in three months she'd put on as many stones, her belly and bum ballooning in size as she stress ate three times her recommended calorific intact. She'd also had to lie to her parents about why she was suddenly working at the other end of the country, told them that she fancied a change of scenery, that was all.

Amanda was excellent at holding grudges, but knew that those responsible for her now being a jumped-up line manager for a second string hotel in a third string town were far beyond her ever being able to get back at... and so head chef Andrew Morgan would have to do as a suitable receptacle for her to drip her bile into.

Every time a guest had even the most minor complaint about what came out of the Crest's kitchen -food a little too cool or over-salted, perhaps- Amanda would grab eagerly and inflate into a drama.

"This may not be the Ivy or the Fat Duck," she would tell Andy, stood in the very centre of the kitchen so that everyone could see and hear, the offending plate of food held high in one hand and her other fist planted in one well-padded hip, "and you may never earn a Michelin star -well, almost certainly with the rather *pedestrian* menu you offer- but could we not, perhaps, *aspire?* Hmm? Maybe something just above the level of a motorway greasy spoon? *Hmm?*"

Andy always had a response, though. The bastard was razor sharp.

"Well, my first instinct is not to trust the culinary expertise of someone who isn't a *bonafide* cook," he had said. "But then again, looking at you, it looks like as far as the gastronomic arts goes you're a really, *really* enthusiastic patron."

When she'd coldly told him she didn't care for his tone, he'd expressed surprise at her attitude;

"It was only a joke, just a bit of banter! Jeepers creepers, I thought us fatties were supposed to be jolly?"

She had raised this last with the assistant manager. Calling her fat was a personal insult and couldn't be tolerated. But the assistant manager was a long term friend of Andy's, and had suggested, given that Andy had included himself in the perceived insult, that is was self-deprecating and therefore not an actionable offence.

Amanda let nothing go. She made a point of performing spot checks, under the guise of health and safety, on the contents of the larders and freezers. Her only success was to find a shrimp that had somehow ended up in a crisper drawer with three heads of romaine lettuce. This cross-contamination she had immediately raised as a major concern with the hotel's manager, especially in light of recent high profile cases in the courts over deaths linked to allergies and the improper labelling of foods.

The manager, a sallow man called Edwards who was close to retirement, had reluctantly agreed that it was serious enough to issue a written warning to the head chef.

Amanda claimed her minor victory by having a light lunch in the hotel's restaurant consisting of a prawn cocktail.

When she finished it, she told the waitress to give her regards to the chef... with the small note that it could have done with just a touch more paprika, and maybe just a hint of Tabasco sauce.

Given this petty victory, she'd laid off the chef for a while, and so wasn't quite certain what to make of his invitation this evening.

He'd collared her in a service corridor when there was no-one else around.

"Mandy," he said. "I think you and me got off on the wrong foot."

"My name is Amanda," she told him. "Or Ms Phelps."

He grinned, held his hands up.

"Oops, sorry, sorry! Anyway, I'm glad I caught you as I just wanted a quick word; and that word is... sorry."

She hadn't expected that.

"Like I said, I reckon we got off on the wrong foot... I'll tell the truth, when you said that my menu was boring, you know, what was it? *Pedestrian.* When you said that it got my back up a bit, only now I've come to realise that what you said only got under my skin because... I agree. I didn't like to admit it, but you were right. It's bloody dull, I've been doing the same safe dishes for ages now, saveloys, chipolatas, and when you said so I got defensive. Reckon I've been a bit lazy."

Amanda was interested in spite of herself... and in spite of the fact that the chef had said *saveloys* and *chipolatas*, which as far as she recalled had never been served at the hotel.

"And...?" she asked.

"Well, I've decided to try a few new things," said the chef. "But I wanted to run them by you first. Sort of a peace offering, but also I know you'll be completely honest about them; you know, being the big boss in the kitchen means my word is God, right? Well, I reckon I need some critical feedback from someone who isn't scared shitless by me, if you'll pardon my French."

She'd thought about it, but really, the appeal to her vanity was too great to say "no", and she had agreed to visit the kitchen after the last dinner sitting and try out any new dishes he had been working on.

He grinned and gave her two thumbs up.

"Over the lips and past the gums!" he'd said.

Which had been a bit odd.

When she let herself in, she frowned.

The whole place was a mess, and deserted.

What the devil was...

Amanda was wrong; the kitchen was not deserted. The head chef had been hiding behind the swing door she had entered.

"Oi, oi, SAVELOY!"

She'd turned to see him, naked, brandishing his cock in one hand and a meat tenderising mallet in the other, which he smashed into her temple.

It went dark.

*****

As consciousness arose, it did so wrapped in the dull brain ache and nausea of a hangover. Which was strange, as Amanda hadn't had a drink since the *indiscretion*.

Stranger still, she was not lying down, but was somehow upright.

Her head throbbed and her shoulders ached as if she had been carrying heavy weights. This, it turned out, was because she was slumped forward in the chair, her wrists tied behind it. Her own weight was the burden that had made her arms ache in their sockets.

She forced herself backward, moaning both with pain and slight relief.

Amanda was in the hotel's kitchen at work. She was sat in front of one of the prep stations, where cooks would assemble the various parts of the diner's meals, ready to be whisked away by the waiting staff. A smooth expanse of steel, splattered with the punctuation of hastily assembled feasts, full stops and commas and exclamation points of dried sauces.

The kitchen.

Yes; of course. She had come in here because... because Andy Morgan the head chef had invited her.

But then what had happened?

Andy stepped into view on the other side of the prep table. He wore a hair net underneath the neat white cap that the kitchen boss wore as a mark of his rank, but otherwise he was naked, his chef's whites and checked trousers nowhere in evidence, his giant cheesy-white gut almost concealing his genitals.

He had a tattoo on his left thigh. It was Tony the Tiger, the Kellogg's *Frosties* mascot. He had one paw wrapped around his giant orange and black striped erection. A speech balloon ran part of the way around Andy's hip. It said; "*MaaaasturBATE!*"

He saw her staring at it.

"Got that in Hua Hin, Thailand" he said. "Same place I met a bar girl who gave me the second best BJ of my life; Urai Irisai her name was."

(*over the lips and past the gums*)

Grinning, Andy laid out his tools in the prep space. A wickedly sharp fillet knife and a pizza cutter.

"Andy, what are you doing?" Amanda asked. Her words were slurred, as if she were drunk.

Andy lent forward and placed a number of items in front of Amanda.

A small glass ice-cream dish, garnished with lettuce. A jar of red powder marked *PAPRIKA*. A bottle of Tabasco sauce.

And strangest of all; two shot glasses.

"I'm tied up," said Amanda. "Why am I tied up? What's happening? What are you doing, Andy?"

Andy said *shhhhh* and gently pressed the tip of one finger to her lips, urging her to be quiet.

"I take all criticism very seriously," Andy said, his tone soft and his grin still splitting his face. "I'll take the hits, I'll roll with them, and I'll come back with a stronger game. But the thing is, nobody around here has been Billy Big Bollocks enough to say shit to me for quite some time... until you did. So this is my way of saying thank you; not only am I going to make you a meal you'll never forget, but I'm going to show you everything I've got..."

(*saveloy*)

He paused.

(*chipolata*)

"This is going to be utterly unique, like nothing any chef has ever done before. And I'm only going to be able to make this once, so you'd better enjoy it. I call this, *hate cuisine.*"

"Andy what are you talking about? Let me go!"

He held his long, limp cock in his left hand. The foreskin was slightly pulled back to reveal soft, crumbly smegma caked under the hood of his glans, as if he had pressed the tip of his dick into brie.

"I've left my shrimp marinating in its own juices for a few days," he told her. "Giving it a cheesy flavour with notes of vinegar. Now, you know the most important part of preparing shrimp? You've got to remove their gut. It tends to contain a lot of grit and sand, not something you want to bite down on."

Amanda was about to speak again -she wasn't sure what she was going to say; she felt a plea behind her lips, perhaps for forgiveness, perhaps for sanity- but then Andy picked up the small knife with the wickedly sharp blade.

His dick slipped into his fist and he pulled his genitals up over the swell of his belly.

"You know, it really does look like a plucked chicken when you do this, doesn't it?" he asked, before sticking the tip of the knife into the juncture between his scrotum and the base of his penis.

Amanda gasped as blood welled and ran along the blade.

Andy winced, still grinning.

"Confession time," he said, his voice just the tiniest bit strained. "Ever since I first set eyes on you I've wanted to stick my cock in your mouth. Girls who like their grub really know how to suck on the old meat-seeking pissile." He began to slice upwards, following the pipeline of his urethra, the hollow tube running the length of the belly of the penis through which urine and sperm pass. Blood flowed freely, rich and dark as a beef *jus* or a cranberry *coulis*. It run down the blade and across Andy's knuckles, then drooled down his scrotum, dripping a puddle into the glass dish with the lettuce. "Bit ironic, really, yeah? All this time I've wanted you to *fellate* me, and now here I am, about to *fillet* myself..."

The blood wiped up and out of the tip of his dick with a flourish, sending drops of blood flicking across the worktop, across Amanda's clothes.

She had found herself unable to move, or speak, or scream. Shock had locked her in place, and prevented her from looking away as Andy dropped the knife to one side so that he could send two fingers wiggling into the incision he had made.

Amanda had been fishing once with her dad, during a holiday in Cornwall. He'd caught a mackerel and tried to show her the best way of gutting it. What Andy was doing was like that; a slit up the belly, then reach in, snag the wormy innards, and rip them straight up and out...

He pulled his urethra out like a length of tiny intestine, flinging even more blood over her.

His grin never broke but sweat stood out in huge jewels all along his receding hairline and agony danced in his eyes.

(*over the lips over the lips*)

Drugs. He had to be on drugs.

"And now," he said in a strained voice. "To serve, Amanda. Tonight you will be enjoying a shrimp *mocktail*with prairie oysters."

He squatted so that he could rest his ruined genitals on the worktop. He carefully spread his testicles to either site of his mangled dick, and then picked up the pizza cutter.

The light glinted on the edge of the sharpened disc of metal.

Amanda finally found her voice, and screamed.

This didn't stop Andy. Starting on the left, he wheeled the blade across the base of his scrotum, right next to where it joined to the inside of his thigh.

Tony the Tiger looked on, still furiously beating his meat.

The blade sliced part of the way through the thick, rubbery skin but then stopped, like a tyre caught in thick mud. Blood started to gush from the wound.

"Huh," whispered Andy in a thick, clogged voice. The sweat was freely pouring down his face now, and his grin was so wide it seemed the corners of his mouth must tear. "Stubborn." He pressed the palm of his free hand down on top of the one that held the pizza cutter's handle, drew the blade back a few inches for a run-up, and ran it across his genitals as hard and as fast as he could.

The blade sliced through him as easily as if his flesh were dough.

The pain made him make a strange, almost chicken-like *"bowwk!"* sound and he stood up, leaving his perfectly severed testicles and penis on the work top.

Amanda screamed and screamed.

(*look how big her mouth is past the gums over the lips and oi oi saveloy*)

Andy threw the pizza cutter away and, with shaking hands, scooped up his manhood. In his fingers it looked like a bird, the chick of some strange featherless freak that had been hit by a car, bloody and dead and limp. He picked up the filleting knife and cut the penis away from the scrotum, slicing through stringy erectile tissue, and dropped the thing into the glass bowl with the lettuce, making sure the glans hung over the edge just like a real prawn would be presented.

With its rumpled flesh of foreskin and its red tip crusted with cheesy smegma, it didn't so much resemble a prawn as a giant maggot, fresh from burrowing in the belly-fat of a corpse.

Andy held the wrinkled, furry sack of his ball bag over one of the shot glasses and carefully decanted half its contents.

The thing that landed in the glass in a sauce of his own blood looked like the eyeball of a creature that had evolved underground for a million years, its sight atrophying into moronic milky dullness. The van deferens tube in the back of it even resembled a severed optic nerve.

Andy decanted his other testicle into the remaining shot glass.

"Prairie oysters," he whispered hoarsely. "Cowboys would eat the balls of the horses they gelded, just tipped them back like a shot of whiskey, like an actual oyster, fresh from the shell. Full of iron. Good for you."

With blood-soaked fingers he indicated the paprika and Tabasco sauce.

"Please," he wheezed. "Season to your own taste. I just have to tidy up a little..."

Amanda had stopped screaming at some point during the horror, her throat too raw and her mind too shell-shocked to keep up the high keening note of maddened fear. Her breathing was low and fast, an unconscious attempt to stop herself passing out. She couldn't look at the "meal" in front of her and found herself watching what Andy did next instead.

She knew what the blow torch was for, of course, though it was seldom used to make *crème brulee* at any other time of year than Christmas.

Andy lit up the specialised catering tool and adjusted the gas with blood-slippery fingers until the roaring flame glowed blue, almost white at its core. Then he began to play the flame across the bleeding crater of sliced flesh between his legs, cauterising the wound with a hiss of sizzling fat and blood and a smell like bacon cooking.

As he played the flickering flame over his ruined flesh, he made a noise like a tea kettle;

"Eeeeeeeeeeeee-"

Evidently, the pain of this was so great that it finally emerged from the haze of whatever drug it was that he was on. The sweat was pouring freely down his entire body in rivulets, his thin hair plastered to his skull. His eyes bulged in their sockets, glistening and unfocused. His grin was a skull grimace with not a trace of humour.

"-eeeeeeeeeeeeeeeeee-"

Amanda shook her head and howled, trying to drown out the horrible noise. This was it, this sound was the cap on everything, the final straw that threatened to send her mind tipping into hysterical, beautiful, merciful madness.

"eeeeeeeeeeeeeeeee!"

And then it was over.

The smell was wonderful, a Sunday morning smell of a full English fry-up, sausages

(*chipolatas and saveloys and over the lips*)

and bacon and black pudding.

Amanda was sobbing, her chest heaving as she struggled to breathe. Her left arm was throbbing and her heart felt like it was caught in between skeletal hands that were squeezing it flat.

Her eyes full of thick tears, she only registered the hotel's head chef as a blurred shape that suddenly began to swell up.

Her eyes were being brushed with coppery smelling knuckles.

Amanda's vision was cleared for her.

Andy was leaning down and looking at her closely, his face less than a foot away from her own. It was perfectly white and absolutely calm. Even the sweat was starting to dry.

He reached down and picked something up.

"You haven't touched your food," he said, his voice a hoarse whisper. The fact that Amanda was restrained didn't seem to occur to him as being adequate reason for why she hadn't. He held up his hand, showed her what was in it, and started to make childish engine noises.

"*Neoowww*," he said. "*Neeeeooww!* Here comes the air-plane... open up the hangar!"

When she didn't, he pinched her nose closed until she had to open her lips to breath... and finally, Andy Morgan got his cock in Amanda Phelps' big fat mouth.

And he made her clean her plate, telling her there were starving children in third world countries who would be glad of having such a feast to swallow. He should know... he'd fed more than a few over the years.

"AT LEAST," said the visitor, her smile still wide in spite of the gruesome facts she had related, *"that is what we have been able to reconstruct of the events."*

Robin's imagination could be a curse as well as a blessing. It had not only allowed for the successful pursuit of a dream career in comics, but it also obsessed in minute detail the worst-case scenario of any life event. This visitor's recitation of facts -drawn from witness testimony, forensic analysis, transcripts of CCTV footage, and more- had been constructed by the creative faculty into an elaborate and thoroughly detailed film projected onto the mind's eye.

Worse was what readers of Robin's work had noted gave it his power; a deeply empathetic understanding of people, even to the point of inhabiting the most vile character's mindsets to make them, if not sympathetic, at least understandable.

This empathy had put Robin right inside Fat Andy's head as he mutilated himself.

"Why?" The voice that asked this was a dry rustle. "Why did he do it?"

The visitor gave a slow shrug, causing the grey hair that cascaded onto her shoulders to rise and fall like a tidal swell.

"We have a very good idea of the mechanism that drove him insane," she said. "But as for his personal mania... well, we all skip to Hell to the beat of our own drum. Chappy had an oral fixation, that's for certain."

"... mechanism that drove him insane?"

She wagged a finger.

"Say now, say now, quid pro quo, right? I've shown you some of mine, you show me a little bit more of yours."

Robin stared at her.

"You want to hear more about the night we made the circle? Why?"

"I told you, I need it to finish my report. The information in and of itself is of no importance -it's all over now, including the shouting- but I pride myself on being thorough. Here, let me pour you a top up. There you go. So, as you were saying...?"

THE CIRCLE
Part Two

BEING SUMMER they didn't need a fire; it was warm and the light was lasting until nearly ten o'clock. Anyway, a fire might have attracted attention. They agreed to make do with torches when it got full dark and they were about their business. They had a pop-up tent each, but it was so warm that Dildo said he was probably going to sleep outside, under the stars, and the others decided this was a bloody good idea.

Fat Andy cooked chipolatas and slices of Kingsmill Toastie on a disposable barbecue he'd picked up in a petrol station on the way and handed them around. He'd brought a cooler for the beer, and from this he produced a bottle of the chipotle & coffee chili sauce he made for his kitchen at work, which he was idly toying with the idea of selling commercially. A simple, frugal meal high on taste and calories, read for the business ahead of them.

"Come on lads," he crowed. "Over the lips and passed the gums, watch out belly here it comes!"

"We don't need to hear about your latest holiday," said Dildo.

"You don't? I thought my tales of dusky maidens sucking my saveloy were savoured by all?"

"Saveloy?" said Shades. "Fuck off!Chipolata at best!"

The plan was to wait until midnight before making their move. They had the gear they needed - planks of wood and precisely measured lengths of rope- all ready to go. They each knew their jobs after practicing over and over in Fat Andy's garden, but on a much smaller scale then what they were going to try tonight. Robin had meticulously figured everything out and made sure they all knew their roles by rote; he had actually done a lot of the maths involved in the process during his last treatment, which had been a pleasant way to while away the time as medical science pumped him full of chemicals.

But whilst they waited for midnight, they had beer.

"A toast!" said Fat Andy, pulling the tab on the top of a can of Fosters.

"To what?" asked Dildo.

Andy shrugged.

"Dunno, really," he said. "Here, Robin, what's that Jewish thing? You say it at weddings and shit. Lack hymen?"

"L'chaim," said Robin. "It means, 'to life'."

"Good enough!" Fat Andy raised his can. "Lack hymen!"

"Lack hymen!" chorused the others.

They drank to it.

Dildo pointed at Shades' drink.

"Not on shift?" he said.

"I swapped with someone else," he said. "Need the Dutch courage for what we're up to."

"Eh? What do you mean?"

"Technically, what we're doing tonight is vandalism."

Dildo blew a raspberry.

"Bollocks, it's art."

"The law wouldn't see it that way."

Fat Andy drained his can, declared "'Nother dead soldier!" and popped open the next..

"It's just squashing down some wheat, or corn, or fucking whatever, to make a naughty picture" he said. "It's not exactly smashing windows or chucking Molotov cocktails. Anyway, thought you answered to a higher authority?"

Shades frowned.

"What's that supposed to mean?"

"Well, even if it is vandalism, is that a sin? It's not like nicking shit, or murder, none of that ten commandment stuff. If it's not a sin, why worry about it?"

"Sin and breaking the law are different. Anyway, Jesus is quite clear on earthly law; render unto Caesar that which is Caesar's. And besides, I'm a bloody prison officer! I'm supposed to be whiter than white! My Jenny would kill me if she knew what we were really doing tonight…"

He'd told his pregnant wife a series of half-truths about why he was getting together with the boys. He'd never lie to her… he had simply omitted details. She knew his friend Robin was dying, and that they were going to help him scrub something off his bucket list… but that was it.

"But you're here anyway, and going to help us."

Shades looked puzzled.

"Of course I am," he said. "Mates stick together." He drained his can. "It's just going to be a little easier if I'm three sheets-faced. 'Nother dead soldier!"

Dildo passed him another can.

He'd told his Dee the whole truth… and ironically, she only half-believed him. She was so paranoid about their relationship, always worried when he went out with the boys that a younger woman would catch his eye.

"I'll drink to that," said Andy.

They did.

Fat Andy belched.

Being free and single, as he put it, he hadn't had to tell anyone what he was up to. He'd simply filed for some holiday he was owed, though that fat bitch had a face like a slapped arse when he'd told her… But fuck her!

(Right in the mouth.)

He belched again, defiant.

Dildo waved a hand in front of his face.

"Phew, spunky!"

Andy gave him the finger. But before he could launch into Dildo over who had the biggest cock, him or his missus, he glanced across at Robin.

He changed tack.

"Oi, face ache, why so glum? Still moping over the loss of your foreskin?"

Robin started, as if someone had prodded him in the side. He'd just been listening to the flow of the banter, but now it looked like he was being dragged in.

He smiled, rolled his beer back and forth between his palms.

"No, I just feel like shit because of the chemotherapy I'm having for the cancer that's fucking killing me. So, 'nother dead soldier!" He threw his empty can into the box they'd set aside, and looked up. His friends wore an interesting mixture of expressions, varying quantities of shock and embarrassment. This made Robin feel good; after years of banter with these beautiful wankers, he finally had a trump card in his hand that beat them all every time. But enough, for now."Also, this beer's fucking shit; who bought it?"

Laughter, a little uneasy, a little relieved.

Eyes turned to Dildo.

"Fuck off, it was on special offer!"

Fat Andy went for the throat.

"So your mum doesn't give you enough pocket money to buy the good stuff, then?"

Dildo's mouth turned into a hard, lipless line. Shades and Robin shared a look.

Fat Andy was the only one who dared this territory.

"Don't call Dee my mum, Andy."

A nibble, a very definite nibble... but Fat Andy still backed away.

"Fine, fine, sorry, say no more. So... how is your husband?"

It was strange; though there were no visible signs to suggest that anything had changed, the atmosphere between the men relaxed. Just the mere hint about the age difference between Dildo and his wife had been enough to cause Robin's muscles to start cramping up, an atavistic response to the danger of the situation, an instinctual flight or fight reaction. Through the years of their friendship, there had been numerous fights, but only a few of them had been deadly serious, the kind of fights that could have irrevocably destroyed their bond of memories. The evening that Dildo had finally relented and brought Dee out to show her off to the boys, something had been said that had kicked off six months of acrimony that had nearly torn them all apart.

Put simply, the age gap between Dildo and Dee was a sore spot not to be touched.

The rest of their relationship, however - particularly the fact that Dildo had small genitals- was fair game.

"*He's* just fine and dandy, Andy, thanks for asking," said Dildo. "*He* let me cum on *his* tits last night."

"Bet she thought a mouse had sneeze on her," said Robin.

Shades giggled.

"No wonder she's the one who wears the trousers in your gaff," said Fat Andy. "She's the only one who's got something to fill them. What the fuck did she say the first time you dropped your skiddies and your nubbin of a knob dropped out?"

In chorus, Shades and Robin said;

"Mine's bigger."

Amidst the laughter, Dildo shrugged.

"It's not what you've got, it's what you do with it, and my Dee has zero complaints in that department. Say's I'm the best shag she's ever had."

"Bitch," said Robin. "She told me the same thing."

"And me," said Shades.

"Twats," said Dildo.

Fat Andy popped another can and held it aloft.

"'Nother dead soldier, and another toast!" he said. "To the lovely Mrs Nash-Smart, and all who sail in her!"

"To Mrs Nash-Smart!" said Robin

"And all who sail in her!" said Shades.

"Cunts," said Dildo, and raised his can. "'Nother dead soldier."

"Here," said Fat Andy, pointing at Robin. "This chemo, does it fuck with your plumbing?"

Only he would have asked.

Dildo and Shades shared a look, eyes wide.

Ever since he had told them Robin had decided to be as honest with his friends about what was happening with him as was possible. Any questions they asked, he would answer as plainly as he could.

Story time…

"I haven't had an erection since it started, no," he said. "Not even a piss hardon first thing."

Fat Andy considered this.

"Have you done any conventions?" he asked.

Of course he'd ask that; as the 'bachelors' of the group it was there job to make the other two jealous with their stories of sexual abandon; Fat Andy would travel to far-flung paradises on his quest to get sucked off by every race on earth, whilst Robin would attend sci-fi and horror conventions and brought back stories of fucking Harley Quins and Wonder Women and even, on one occasion, a threesome involving a Care Bear and an Ewok.

He'd said he got them both to suck him off at the same time, without taking their costumes off, and labelled that tale the Teddy Bear's Dick Lick.

"I gave up the circuit ages ago," he said. "It was always exhausting."

"What's exhausting about signing a few comic books and banging fan-girls?"

Robin decided whether to answer honestly.

"Have you ever signed your own name five hundred times in three hours?" he asked. "You can't even make a fist to wank with afterwards; those girls were providing a service. Anyway, it's not just signing, you also have to talk to the freaks and mouth-breathers, and they all ask the same stupid bloody questions, or try to get me interested in their idea for a comic, telling me if I write and draw it for them I can have half the money..."

"That's a nice way to talk about the people buying your work," said Dildo.

Robin shrugged.

"Oh, some of them are okay, but let's face it, the kind of people who want to read the kind of gory ultra-violence I pen? Absolute fucking freaks."

"And what does that make you, if you're the one writing it?"

He shrugged again.

"I'm just working through my own issues. But instead of paying a headshrinker for the privilege, people pay me. Fuck 'em."

This earned a pause in proceedings.

Beer was consumed whilst mulling over was going on.

Shades asked who had the time?

They had hours yet. Plenty of time for a few more beers and a lot more banter. The sun stretched their shadows out behind them on the hill and the horizon was turning that streaky shade of magenta that meant the next door would be a scorcher. *Red sky at night...*

"Do you have a name yet?" Robin asked Shades.

Shades held his hand out palm down and see-sawed it.

"Easier to ask if we've whittled our list down to a dozen possibilities," he said. "Boys and girls."

"You could cut the list in half if you just went with unisex names," said Dildo.

"That's no good," said Fat Andy. He broke open another beer to punctuate his point. "That just means it'll have the piss ripped out of it all the way through school, like we used to with dear Robin Red-Breasts here. You remember that, bob bob bobbin', how we used to rip the fuck out of you for having a girl's name? 'Nother dead fucking soldier!"

"What flavour are you hoping for?" Robin asked.

Shades shrugged.

"Doesn't matter, so long as it's healthy."

"Bollocks," said Dildo. "Everyone says that, and it's not true, it's just being superstitious, like the kid would be born deformed or something just because you said you wanted a boy more than anything."

"That's true," said Fat Andy. "Look what happened to Dildo's parents, they said they wanted a boy, and they got something which only looks like a boy, until you drop his skiddies."

"Excuse me," said Dildo, "isn't it time we got back to making fun of Robin's junk because his parents chopped the end off it? Or that shrimp thing you've got?"

Fat Andy grabbed his crotch.

"That's no shrimp, that's a cucumber!"

"Fucking smells like shrimp; *gone off* shrimp."

"And what the fuck is that supposed to mean?"

Robin raised an eyebrow. Dildo did too.

It wasn't even very good bait, but Fat Andy hadn't just bitten, he'd *chomped.* He had snapped those words and he was glaring hard at Dildo; the can in his hand was dented from his grip suddenly tightening.

And Fat Andy *never took the bait.*

"Fishy," said Dildo. "The joke was saying your cock smells fishy, like bad seafood. What the fuck did you think I meant?"

For a moment, Fat Andy's glare was hard, livid. Then he shook his head.

"Nothing, nothing," he said. "It's just a work thing; there's this new bitch in charge of hospitality and she's got it in for me, keeps trying to make out my kitchen is lax in the old hygiene department. It's nothing."

He mused, then added as an afterthought;

"Big fat bitch.Wouldn't mind getting her to suck me off."

He sank his beer and pitched the can.

"'Nother dead soldier."

"A girl," said Shades.

"You want a girl?" said Robin.

Shades shrugged.

"Florence," he said. "A little girl called Florence. I'd read her *Alice in Wonderland* and build her a Wendy house and not let her know about the internet and social media or any of that shit until childhood was over."

He sighed.

"But then again," he continued, "I get to thinking about the kind of scum I work with... You know that expression, 'hate the sin, not the sinner'? That goes neatly with another one, 'the Lord never gives us more than we can handle.' My job is like a rock and a hard place, you know, except it's those two little expressions instead. There are men on my wing who I don't even want to think of as men, because of the things they've done..." he paused; he couldn't say it, but he could,"to *children*. You remember a few years back, that bloke who used to be a Lollipop Man? Sick scum like that. And I think about a little girl called Florence growing up in a world with those kinds of men in it."

He said this with such sincerity and understated feeling that it created an awkwardness in the banter-flow.

"Don't even know why we bother locking them up," said Dildo. "Ought to just castrate the fuckers."

Shades shrugged.

"Vengeance is mine, saith the Lord," he quoted. "Men don't get to decide the fate of men."

But before he could expound on this theme and derail some class-A banter entirely, Fat Andy came to the rescue.

"If it's a boy you should call it Jeff, after his granddad," he said. "And if it's a girl, call it Gina after her grandmother."

Robin smiled. He knew where this was going.

Dildo was frowning. He didn't.

"But those aren't my mum and dad's names..." said Shades doubtfully.

"Nah," said Andy. "They're mine."

One, two, three...

The penny dropped.

"Twat!" said Shades.

A few 'nother soldiers bit the bullet.

Fat Andy lay back against his rucksack, breaking open another can and draining most of it as he went down.

"Actually, when I have kids, I'm going to be all fucking cool and give them really wanky names that they'll change when they grow up," he said, and belched. "Like verbs, or colours. Vermilion for a boy, and Dancing if it's a girl."

"How many tins have you had?" asked Dildo.

Fat Andy shrugged.

"I'm not as think as you drunk I am," he said.

"How about you?" said Shades, turning to Robin.

"How about...?"

"What are you going..." Shades stopped talking when he realised what he was saying, and to who.

Robin cocked his head to one side.

Shades didn't know what to say.

"Dee says she doesn't want kids," Dildo said, cutting in, salvaging the banter. "She says there's too many humans in the world already. Not too keen on humans, is my missus."

"... or German names," said Fat Andy to himself. "Like Wilhelm, and... and... shit, Wilhelmina..."

"Ginger," said Robin. "I'm with you Shades. Whenever I thought about it, I thought I'd like a little girl. I'd have called her Ginger." He drained his beer, and a wave of nausea blew through him. He rode it out, and when he opened his eyes again his friends were all looking at him in the dying light of the day, the sky shading from magenta around the edges of the distant trees and the fields to purple above the gently swaying treetops to black overhead, their eyes in shadows. "I'd have called her Ginger."

Right then, he could have saved them. What swept through him at that moment was not nausea as only moments before, but exhaustion, that kind of soul-flatness which is the true form of depression; why bother, why were they doing this, what was the point? He could have just said, fuck this, and left, and gone home to wait until it was time to go into the hospital one last time... and if he had done so they all would have been saved.

But his love for his stupid, impossible, dickhead friends won out. It told him that this wasn't for him, this was for them... and they were worth the final titanic effort of giving a shit.

He snapped his fingers and pointed at the beer stash.

"I'm not nearly pissed enough to be this moody," he said. "Let's get shit faced and draw a cock and balls so big you can see 'em from fucking space. 'Nother dead soldier!"

"YOU AND your friends," said his visitor, who still hadn't given a name, "are what my daughter would call textbook examples of toxic masculinity. She's what you might call 'woke', you see, and likes giving me these little lectures about diversity and representation and all that sort of woolly nonsense."

She paused, her mouth pursing as she considered something.

"Mind you, if chappies like your dead chums are the calibre of male available to her generation, it's really no wonder she's a rug muncher."

Robin looked closely again at the visitor, saw the rainbow flag pin in her lapel, and suddenly everything was far too weird and far too real.

This strange woman claimed to be some sort of a spy or a hired killer, working for one of the world's largest biotech companies. She had said, as easily as explaining the story line from last night's episode of a soap opera, that Fat Andy had cut off his own penis and testicles and force fed them to the woman he had been bitching about the night of the crop circle. She had a grown-up daughter who was gay and whom she showed support to by clearly identifying herself as a LGBT+ ally.

And I'm sat here in a hospital bed, with a jar of sunflowers next to me from my mum, having to get my head around this insanity.

"I read some of your comics," said the woman with the long grey hair in the powder blue trouser suit.

"You read some of my comics," Robin repeated.

"Yes, for my research about you. I like to know all about my subjects, and what people choose to do for work often tells me lot."

"And what does my work say about me?"

She sniffed.

"Well, firstly, that drawing and writing your own ongoing comic title is incredibly labour intensive, which may explain the fact that I have been unable to unearth any sort of history of personal relationships. You have your work, your mother and step-father, and the occasional evening out with your dear childhood chums... and that's it. So I might surmise that the nature of your art means you don't have time to pursue a fulfilling, deeper connection with another human being... or I might surmise otherwise, such as it makes a good excuse for not telling the truth."

Robin stared at her.

"As for the comics themselves... ghastly nonsense with a superficial veneer of cleverness that certain people might mistake for actual intelligence. Such as calling your main protagonist, a transitioning metahuman, Ophelia Gynist... Miss O. Gynist? Oh, how bloody witty! What a larf!*"*

Robin' cheeks began to burn as blood rushed into them.

"Turning the gender tropes of the superhero genre on their head is a bit of a one trick pony, isn't

it? How often can you stuff a male in a fridge with a knowing wink, hmm? But I suppose it's easier than true originality. Oh don't look at me like that! This is constructive criticism, and anyway…" she said, her eyes narrowing even as her smile widened, "the only reason what I am saying hurts is because you know it's true, don't you?"

Couldn't say anything.Couldn't trust to say anything.

"Say now, say now," she continued. "Quid pro quo and all that; what do you want to know?"

"The field," Robin said, tightly. "Tell me about the field. What does it have to do with what happened to my friends?"

The visitor regarded the patient, the target, coolly for a moment.

"Lab work will only get you so far," she said. "Eventually you have to test theories in the real world. We own pockets of land here and there all over the world, often in out-of-the-way areas, sometimes close to major population centres… luckily, the field you and your chums chose for your little joke was one of the former, and as such, the fallout has been easy to contain. Essentially, we were growing a modified form of winter wheat that had been altered so that it would form a more bonding relationship with the network of sub-soil fungi that parasitize it; this would allow for a much greater uptake of nutrients. It appears we were too successful, as it formed a secondary relationship with an entirely different fungi, one which we would never seek to encourage."

"A secondary... wait, so this was a genetically modified crop? Aren't those illegal?"

"Bit of a grey area, that. Almost all food grown and consumed by humans has been altered at the genetic level by years of selective breeding. All we do is cut out the bit where a dozen generations pass."

"But what has that got to do with..."

"Have you heard of the mass witch panics of the medieval period?" she asked suddenly. "Whole communities across Europe went crazy, thought they saw women riding through the skies on broomsticks, thought that the Devil held masses in the woods at which babies were sacrificed. A collective mania that saw over five million women over a period of ten years burnt to death."

She shifted in her chair.

"There have been other mass panics and insanity, of course, like the dancing disease that caused people to boogie until they dropped dead of exhaustion. It was an idea that started going around and around in people's heads..."

She shrugged.

"Fat Andy got the idea into his head that he simply had to mouth-fuck a woman he worked with, and it got all jumbled up in his head with food... and your friend Dildo, well... he had a bit of a hang up about his, hmm, manhood..."

DILDO
Bigger & Better

DEE NASH-SMART had a number of anxieties, just like any other woman, and just like any other woman she had become adept at handling them along with the rest of the shit the world liked to throw her genders' way every day. Her main method of dealing with her worries was to shove them down and slap a "hard bitch" facade on top, but every now and again something would rise to the surface...

Every aspect of her life had its own set of worries, and they could for the most part be neatly partitioned. Any worries she had about her professional career, for example, were entirely different beasts to those she had about her appearance; she had successfully kept her ambitions far away from the way she felt about her height and flat chest, for example. But there was always going to be some overlap, and where that overlap occurred individual niggles could combine, put their strength together, and rise up from her subconscious to speak clear, crisp, and terrible words in her waking ear.

The biggest overlap was, naturally, her closest personal relationship.

Dillon Nash-Smart was not only eighteen years younger than her, he was also, theoretically, an employee. And yet, somehow, despite misgivings over professional conduct and ethics, and despite her anxieties about being taller than him, older than him, successful and respected... *and the fact that he was absolutely gorgeous, why would he look twice at a Plain Jane like her...* somehow love had grown.

They had made a good life. Dee didn't know quite how much of this was based on shoving her fears over their obvious differences down out of sight, out of mind, but she was aware that they were only just below the surface of her conscious mind, and were easy to trigger.

It had only been a week since her initial, nose-twitching scent of something wrong, but she had already convinced herself that he was seeing someone else. It had started when he had insisted on taking over the late shift from Ellen, choosing to spend nights at the practice caring for the animals overnight rather than at home with her. Actually, this wasn't true; if she was going to pin a date on when she first thought something was wrong, she would have put it back to a month before, when he and his friends had gone and made that childish crop "circle."

But Dee was wrong in believing that the man known as Dildo to his friends was seeing someone else.

Quite the opposite in fact. He was working on himself.

For her.

This was why he had insisted on taking on the late shifts recently, something he hadn't *really* had to do since they had gotten married. It was actually a perk, though barely acknowledged, that Dillon as a glorified dogsbody didn't have to take any of the gruelling overnight shifts that came up whenever they had to keep one or more pets in for observation and care. Either Ellen or Cy, both of whom were technically more qualified than Dillon, or any work-experience kid on a year internship would have to take these duties on, with the junior practice partner's husband only picking up the odd night here and there as a sop.

Everyone who worked at Crest Valley Vets were dedicated members of the team, but having to force medication down the throats of sick pets who found themselves in a scary environment several times a night was not something anyone looked forward to, a combination of boredom mixed with scratches and bites and vast amounts of clean-up, of wee, and poo, and pus and blood.

Dee had asked him why he had decided to take on the better part of a week's worth of looking after a Labrador recovering from stomach surgery after it had eaten several of those plastic scoops used for measuring out washing detergent gel. Dillon explained that he had grown a personal attachment to the dog in question, an animal whose owner's had seen fit to call Raffles.

"And anyway, I think... I think Cy and Ellen are really starting to resent me coasting," he said.

"What do you mean?" Dee had asked.

She knew what he meant. But it was odd to hear it from him; one of the acknowledged aspects of his character was the fact he was a mild sociopath. He loved animals, but didn't give a shit about people.

Well, except her, and those stupid "mates" of his...

"The fact that late shift's should be on a rotating time table, but I've been able to skip out on it because I'm fucking the hot cunt who's in charge round here," said Dillon.

Dee had felt her cheeks heat a little. And so an untruth slipped through.

There are many reasons for human attraction, as infinitely complex and unique as a snowflake, and here was a small part of what made Dillon and Dee's unlikely union possible; Dillon was, at heart, a dirty little boy... and Dee had a deeply repressed dirty little girl inside her.

She'd tried to be professional, and voiced the rationale they had both used to excuse that which they both knew was true, that it really wasn't on that Dillon was able to exploit his position... but then he'd shut her up by unzipping the front of her sensible work jeans and sliding three fingers up inside her.

This conversation had been taking place during a stock check of the medical supply room. Anyone could have walked in on them, anyone could have caught them, as Dillon expertly slipped his fingers in and out and rubbed her clit with the heel of his thumb, his free hand cupping one of her small breasts as he leaned up to kiss her.

So Dillon had taken on seven nights in a row of looking after the blonde Labrador who had a taste for Persil flavoured plastic, and to give Dee her credit, it wasn't until the fourth night she started to worry.

He'd become quiet. But she could surely put that down to tiredness, as he was snatching sleep only where he could in the evening, in those hours between his day work and his night duties.

He'd become less affectionate... this was harder to reason away as exhaustion, as not only did the sly and naughty gropes at work cease, but also those smaller though no less important caresses, a hand touch here or a peck on the cheek there.

After the second night, he even took to sleeping in the spare room, the one they kept for guests as it would never belong to a child of theirs. He said the evening light bothered him in their West facing room, even with the blinds drawn.

Dillon even became slack about his appearance.

Normally he dressed well and groomed himself thoroughly. Dee had once accused him (only half in jest, if she were honest) that he kept himself as if he were still on the market. Dillon's response had been perfect; he'd told her he loved being her toy-boy, and wanted her to be able to show him off. The response had been perfect in that Dee was able to make a mental shift, burying her worry about their age difference under an outward facade of treating him like a trophy, of seeming to *revel* in the fact that she had landed someone much younger and so good looking. She took him shopping, and would wait outside the changing rooms of the high-end clothing shops whilst he tried on outfits for her to select.

But as the days of the night shifts went on Dillon chose to wear shapeless, baggy clothes, loose tracksuit bottoms and jumpers, the kinds of things he only wore when doing decorating or walking the dogs. She had briefly mentioned this, and he said that as he was spending almost all of his time at the practice it made sense; if he wasn't getting covered in the various substances that came out of sick animals -Raffles had developed nervous diarrhoea, for one- then he was getting covered in the cleaning fluids he had to use to maintain a sterile environment.

Dee accepted this. His old, worn out Nike tracksuit bottoms were piebald with splashes of bleach.

But then there was a smell. It was faint, but she picked up on it whenever she got close to him. Underneath his Mont Blanc aftershave, barely masked by Lynx Africa roll-on deodorant, there was a gassy, sweetly *rotten* scent coming from beneath his baggy clothing.

All of this combined should have suggested that her husband having an affair was an unlikely proposition. But her fears about the age gap, and about her own awkward body which she had never felt at ease with until Dillon's mad lust for it, began to speak louder and louder.

And anyway... what else could be going on that meant he kept himself away from her, if it wasn't that he was keeping himself for another?

On the evening of the seventh day, she waited until he got up from his after work sleep, ready to head back to the practice and take over the late care, and she confronted him.

"Dillon, before you go, I have to... I want to talk."

She had been waiting on the landing, just outside the door of the spare bedroom.

He yawned. He was already dressed, wearing those same bleach-splashed tracksuit bottoms he'd been in all week.

"Sure, talk about what?" he asked.

Dee didn't really do subtlety. And she was hurting.

"Why are you avoiding me?"

Dillon gazed at her.

"Don't play daft, you know that's what you're doing. If it was just some sense of guilt making you punish yourself by taking on every late shift, that would have been suspicious enough; you don't do guilt."

He shrugged. He was a little sociopathic, sure.

"Maybe so, yeah, but I told you, the guys have been resenting it, and I could do without the hassle of..."

She held a hand up. Obediently he stopped talking.

"We've been married two years. In that time you've done maybe a fortnight of lates in total.

You've been quite happy for me to use my influence to fudge the schedule up until now and not given two shits about the way Cy and Ellen may have felt. "

Dillon scratched under his arm. There was a brief burst of the stench of stale sweat.

"Okay," he said. "But why are you bringing this up now? You could have called bollocks the moment I said I was..."

"Because a lot of the time, I want to believe what you tell me," she told him. "You know that, and you know that I know you do."

He stared at her.

"Tell me Dillon," she said. "What is going on?"

He swallowed thickly, ran a hand through his hair.

He looked frustrated, but somehow happy too. Naughty, found out.

"Fine! I'm not ready yet but... I suppose I can give you a sneak preview of what your future looks like!"

And so saying, he gingerly pulled down his tracksuit bottoms to show her what he had done.

The thing between his legs wasn't the small yet perfectly formed set of genitals that she knew and loved, the equipment that, though lacking in dimension, was more than made up for by its owner's endurance, enthusiasm, and endlessly mucky mind. What was there now had no frame of reference for her; Dec's mind flashed pictures of bunches of rotting fruit, grotesquely swollen and overripe and leaking stickiness. Her next thought was that he had been horribly injured, that someone had beaten his penis and testicles with a crowbar; how else to explain how they were so enormously swollen yet sickly looking, a spongy mass of purple and blue bruises and seeping wounds? His cock was a huge, misshapen cucumber in the advanced stages of rot, sticking straight up against his belly to his chest, and his scrotum was as big as a sagging watermelon, bloated with putrescent decay, dangerously shiny, the skin distended with pus that oozed from an ugly looking crusted black scar.

That scar wasn't the only black. Threads of blackness like forked lightning spread all over his genitals and radiated up onto his stomach, climbing, up to his navel... infection, nasty, nasty infection, spreading.

He had a tropical disease. Dee thought; *elephantiasis, I've seen pictures of those afflicted, that must be what...*

And yet his fingers went down to touch himself, tenderly, wincing a little.

One hand cradled his scrotum. The way it flopped over his palm made her think of the bags responsible dog owners collected their pet's shit in, full to bursting with doggy diarrhoea. Dillon wrapped his other hand around the bloated tip of what was his penis, that giant rotten cucumber that was erect against his flat and hairless belly. He squeezed.

Something that stank of fish and had the consistency and colouring of chunky vomit oozed out of the crusty end.

It splattered onto the landing carpet between them.

"I wanted to wait until it was all healed up," he said. "What do you think? Big, ain't it? And I did all the work myself!"

*****

Of course he'd cared for Raffles, as well as a guinea pig with a broken leg that had come in mid-week, but the main reason Dillon had wanted to take over the night shifts was so that he would be alone, with full access to the surgery.

He'd begun by working on his balls.

(*thought a mouse had sneeze on her*)

He'd administered a local aesthetic and waited until he was sure he was numb. He'd tested by pinching the thick, rubbery skin of his scrotum together, and then pushed a sewing needle through the wad of flesh.

He'd felt the metal sliver pass in and out of himself, but it didn't hurt.

He sat himself on the stainless steel table, arranging his tools on his right. The yellow haz-mat bucket was to his left, as he wouldn't need that just yet.

He had a hose and face mask that would normally be used to administer aesthetic to the animal under surgery. He put the mask on and it only just covered his mouth, leaving his nose free, but he did not attach the end of the tube to a tank. He breathed through his nose. No problem. He held the plastic tube in front of his palm and blew hard into the mask; air puffed onto the middle of his hand.

Dillon picked up a scalpel. He breathed through his nose.

He pinched his scrotum again, and made a quick cut about an inch long in it, just deep enough to breach through the skin but not so deep as to cut into the *tunica vaginalis*, the fatty tissue that sheathed his testes.

He dropped the scalpel and pushed the end of the tube into the bleeding slit he had made. He pinched the skin closed around it.

Then he began to blow into the face mask, drawing in air through his nose and then exhaling out hard through his mouth.

Doing this, he forced air into his scrotum.

It began to inflate like a balloon, swelling from a small, neat bag the size of a single hen's egg into a wobbling roundness the size of a tennis ball.

It was working.

Bigger.

He kept breathing in through his nose and breathing out through his mouth until his ball bag was as big as a large grapefruit, his cock a small pink stalk sticking up from the base. The skin had begun to turn shiny by being stretched, with capillaries quite clearly visible between pubic hair which grew further apart as he inflated himself.

Bigger.

He had to squeeze tighter around the base of the tube, pinching the skin airtight, and he had to breathe harder to force more air into himself. The natural elasticity of his scrotal sack was being pushed far beyond what it was used to. He knew there was no danger of bursting, but it was resisting more as the pressure inside increased.

When the jiggling air bladder attached to his crotch was the size of a honeydew melon he decided to stop.

He pulled the tube out with a bloody, sucking little sound, his pinching fingers snapping tight on the cut.

With his other hand he cupped himself.

Huge.

Good.

His original idea had been to induce a *hydrocele testis* in himself, to try and force the extra space to fill with serosal fluid, but he had realised that would take too long. Instead, Dillon decided on stretching himself out first, making his scrotum as baggy as possible before stuffing the empty space with material.

For the first three nights, this was what he did, inflating his scrotum to an obscene size, holding the air in, and then releasing it, over and over, stretching out his ball bag. When he was finished he used a sticking plaster to cover the wound, not wanting to seal it because then he would just have to cut it open again.

During the day he munched codeine tablets for the pain and did a pretty good job of imitating his normal, non-insane self.

On the fourth night he began the stuffing.

The issue of what exactly he could stuff his enlarged ball bag with had at first been a conundrum. He had thought he could remove material from some other part of his body and use that, like the way excess fat could be removed from the buttocks and injected into the lips to plump them up for the "bee-sting" look; unfortunately he had a distinct lack of surplus subcutaneous blubber, which would have been ideal to liposuction out and then squirt into his nut-sack.

It was whilst assisting Dee on the operation with Raffles that he realised he had ready access to plenty of organic material he could use in his augmentation.

(*wears the trousers*)

Fingers still pinching closed the slit in his scrotum, his free hand opened the plastic hazardous material container on his left hand side. It was yellow and red, about the size of a picnic cooler, and was clearly marked as biological material that was to be incinerated.

Anatomical waste.

He fumbled it open one handed, and held his breath as it exhaled a stench that was a mixture of butcher-shop and sewer, almost sweet, a smell you could nearly taste in the back of your throat, like just after vomiting when half-digested chunks of food get caught behind your soft palette.

The contents were mostly material excised during operations, but there were also a few limbs taken from amputations, and a few whole animals; it was standard practice to assure owners whose pets died or were put to sleep that they would have the cremated remains returned to them, but what actually happened was that after a week owners would be contacted to collect a bag of ashes that were scraped up from a mass incineration... so technically, what they took home would by the law of averages contain a certain amount of the carbonised remnants of their beloved animal.

To Dillon's sickened, addled, hallucinating mind, it didn't matter where the material came from -alive, dead, a different species- as long as it was All Organic.

He pulled out a length of what looked like well chewed tripe, a glistening yellow-white mat like bubble wrap smeared with clotted blood. Some of Raffle's stomach lining.

Dillon had asked for a magic kit for Christmas when he was a kid, and had received one that had about a dozen different props for performing the basic sleights that any magician should know. It had been a phase when he was about eleven, and he'd been convinced he'd be brilliant at it, until Fat Andy had suggested that all magicians were bum-bandits and that anyone who wanted to become one must be, by default, a shirt-lifting poof.

One of the tricks had been making a handkerchief vanish. You made a fist and, using one finger, poked the hanky into it, stuffing the fabric in with a few deep prods; really what he were doing was tucking it into a false thumb, a hollow prosthetic that your real thumb would then slide into to conceal the contents, before flourishing an open palm that was empty of any sign of a snot-rag, ta-dah!

Inserting the sick dog's excised stomach lining into his scrotum was like poking the handkerchief into that false thumb. Poke, poke, poke.

(*got something to fill them*)

He reached back into the medical waste container for more material, rooting around in sticky, squelching masses of sliced muscle and skin and slimy fat.

His hand closed on something that felt like a fuzzy, bony ball.

It was a hamster, a Russian Giant. Its fur was matted into crazy spikes with blood and other body fluids. Its back was hunched up, the way hamsters get when they are very old, and its dead eyes were open, staring at eternity.

Dillon stuffed it into his scrotum.

Next he pulled out a handful of tumours that looked like a cluster of glossy white toadstool caps trailing ribbons of phlegmy connective tissue, and topped with something like an obscene grape; two days ago someone had brought in their Maine Coon, a big old cat that had been in a scrap with a young rival. They hadn't been able to save the eye, and so they had to excise it. Cats eyes change shape depending on the time of the day, and the fact that the dead iris was wide open indicated that the fight must have happened about midnight.

He crammed the cat's eye and the cancerous tumours into himself.

Dillon continued the process of packing until he was satisfied. Rotten hide and neatly incised arteries kept poking out of the slit in his scrotum; he was full to overflowing.

His task done, he sealed himself up with medical staples.

Dillon rested his hands on the huge bulk between his thighs. It was horribly bruised, mottled with filthy purple and polluted yellow, and had the heft and texture of an overfilled dog shit bag, but it would settle and heal. The main thing was, he was Billy Big Bollocks.

He could now work on the second part of his genital augmentation; the stumpy nub of his cock looked out of place sticking up from the hugeness of the rest of him, but that was okay. Unlike his old friend Robin Wasser, Dillon was a Cavalier, not a Round Head, and had plenty of foreskin to work with... as well as the amputated rear leg of a pure bred miniature poodle called Wilberforce Midsummer-Nocturne, whose owners simply called him Willy.

*****

"What the hell have you done to yourself?" whispered Dee.

Dillon wagged his sickening erection from side to side. It made muffled clicking sounds, like someone cracking their knuckles, and a half dozen stitches close to where it joined his scrotum ripped with a squirt of black blood.

"Eleven inches of meat," Dillon said. "It's all for you, babes. And just look at these balls, you know you want this fat sack slapping your arsehole whilst I'm slamming this massive cock into your guts!"

No she did not. She didn't want the awful, diseased mess of suppurating flesh anywhere near her. The smell alone was enough to make the gorge rise in her throat. His dirty talk had always inflamed her before, but that was when he'd been parading naked before her with his own neat, pretty little cock and balls, not this monstrous... thing.

She stepped backwards.

Dillon's fingers skimmed along the bottom of the mottled shaft, and she saw that there was a patch of *fur* holding one half of its length to the other. In fact... the entire thing was a patchwork of different flesh, inexpertly stitched together with surgical staples.

Dillon had, in fact, hollowed out the long femur of a dog's leg as if he were making a flute from it, and this he had forced down the eye of his own penis, forcing it into his urethra and causing his glans to split. This bone had formed the core of his extension, around which he had packed more material from the haz-mat bin until it looked like a hellish version of the "elephant's leg" in a kebab shop, from which doner meat was sliced. Then he had patiently wrapped the thing in skins and stapled them in place, using twice as many staples around the base so that the whole thing fused with his own flesh.

"I'm going to turn you inside-fucking-*out*," he growled.

"Dillon," Dee said, "Dillon, please tell me this is a joke, please tell me that's not really you."

He lunged for her.

Dee's hands shot out on reflex, smacking into his shoulders, pushing him away.

Dillon stumbled back.

Dee turned and, sobbing, ran back along the landing, heading for the stairs.

She might have been bigger than him, but he was young and fast. Dillon tackled his wife, and brought them both crashing down in front of the airing cupboard, knocking the wind out of Dee and smashing her jaw against the carpeted floor so hard three of her teeth cracked and she bit off the tip of her tongue.

The shock of the fall and the sudden flaring pain in her mouth blunted Dee's instinct to defend herself, and Dillon was kneeling on her calves and had already ripped her jeans down her thighs before she tried to thrash him off.

"*Geddoffmuh!*" she cried, spitting blood and the chunk of her bitten tongue. "*Geddufuggoffmuh!*"

"Doggy style it is, then!" Dillon crowed, and laughed as if this were just their usual boisterous bedroom games.

Fingers ripped her sensible white underwear to one side, and then something unnatural was pressed into the cleft of her buttocks, something large and sticky like a rotting toadstool. Dillon was grunting rapidly, lust making him clumsy as he tried to use his newly altered and unwieldy genitals.

The toadstool slid into Dee's reluctant rectum lubricated with its own decaying fluids. The heavy, sagging thing that balloon below it slid across the tops of the backs of her thighs, leaving a trail of clotted blood.

His entering took her breath away.

Dillon had asked her many times before to do anal, and she had always refused. But his cock before wouldn't have felt like this, beer can thick and slimy, like the hugest shit she had ever taken.

Dee shuddered, her whole being suddenly concentrated around this violation.

Then she lost her fucking mind.

Screeching with horror and disgust, her hands were flat on either side of her and she was pushing up and twisting with her whole body, flipping herself over, her strength and weight suddenly pitched to singular purpose.

In the blur of motion and violence there was a core, still centred around the intrusion into her rectum, which allowed her to feel something inside her snap.

Not her. Nothing of hers.

The thing in her arse. That had snapped.

Dillon let out a weird yodelling noise, a sound of sudden shock and pain. Instinctively he retreated, and Dee felt the huge mass of warped flesh slide out of her.

She almost thought she heard a wet *pop* as the tip exited her anus.

She crawled forward, dragging herself on her elbows and knees until she reached the head of the stairs and dared look back.

Dillon's face was pure white, glazed with sweat.

The thing in his hands had a right angle in it, and a huge split had opened along the length of the shaft, exposing the wet bone inside. It looked like a baby's arm had been broken, and the baby had been dead for a month, dead and decaying.

"Look what you did," he whispered. "Look what you did! All my work! You broke my fucking dick!"

Dee had pulled herself to her feet and was breathing hard, staring at her husband.

Anger and hatred flooded through her with such strength and intensity that she felt her blood shaking inside her. That was the only way to describe the sensation of rushing adrenaline, that her blood was quaking with rage.

Dillon had tried to rape her. He'd tried to *rape her*.

It was a simple fact, and before that terrible evening she wouldn't have been able to say what her reaction to such a scenario would have been. She felt dirty. She felt disgusted. She felt violated.

She hated him and she wanted to hurt him.

Dee's left leg almost gave under her as she paced forward -Dillon had put most of his weight onto pinning that calf down- but she managed to stay standing with an awkward lurch.

He didn't think to defend himself, he wasn't even looking. All his attention was focused on his broken cock. He flexed it at its "elbow" and animal muscle slithered out of its belly.

Dee used her momentum, and kicked her husband between his splayed thighs as hard as she could, as if the motley balloon of flesh resting on the floor was a football and she was taking a penalty.

He exploded.

The abused skin of his scrotum burst in long, ragged seams from which burst forth streamers of necrotic tissue, a gush of stinking black and scarlet and grey and purple filth, stringy meat and glossy fat and wormy arteries, tiny sad skeletons and excised cancerous nodules. It sprayed across the floor and Dillon's thighs and up his chest and flecks spewed up Dee's legs as if she had stomped in a bucket of offal in an abattoir.

Her foot was stuck halfway into his groin, buried in the avalanche of dead animal flesh.

Idly, she wiggled her toes. Her toenails scraped against his testicles.

Dee looked at her husband. Dillon looked at his wife.

Just like any couple that were deeply in tune with one another. They even finished each other's screams.

SOUL SICKNESS, a nausea that painkillers could not help with. Robin wasn't a spiritual person -when was I last in a synagogue? My Bar Mitzvah? And even back then I felt like a fraud- but after hearing the clinical and dispassionate explanation for what Dillon had done to himself, it was almost possible to believe in a soul; it seemed as though there was something inside Robin felt sick, as if there truly were an eternal spirit and it wanted to vomit.

"How..." Nausea, a wave. Swallowed thickly. "How can you sit there and tell me this stuff and not puke?"

She shrugged.

"I didn't know the chap personally. No emotional connection."

She poured another glass of Lucozade.

"Here you go, wet your whistle. I believe you have a little bit more to tell me yet, and then I'll finish telling you what I know."

"You still haven't explained about the field," Robin said.

"Oh, does it really matter?" she asked him. "And anyway, I've promised to tell you about what happened to your chums, isn't that enough quid for your quo?"

"It's all part and parcel." Words snapped; angry. "What they did, and why they did it. That was the deal, the whole truth."

She sighed theatrically, as if she had a thousand better things to do in a million other places.

"Fine! So now, so now, where was I? I told you that the crop you lot disturbed was an experiment, yes? We bred a variety of wheat which would create a much stronger arbusularmycorrhizac bond with naturally occurring soil based fungi, in an attempt to enhance an already beneficial relationship; the wheat provides the fungi with ten to twenty percent of the CO2 they draw from the air, and in return the fungi exchanges this for anything up to eighty percent of the phosphorous the plant requires from the soil. A win-win, a mutually gratifying scenario occurring naturally; we wanted to give this a bit of a boost, which would help cut down on the amount of fertiliser required per growing period and increase yield. Unfortunately, we were a little too successful, and boosted the growth rate of a different parasitic-fungus... a nasty little blight called ergot."

Science had never been Robin's strong suit but that name rang a distant bell deep in memory... research for a past story? Yes.

"I told you about the witches, about how people saw them flying, about the fear and paranoia that swept through communities like a collective madness that made them put to death innocent old crones. These episodes happened

during particular periods, times in which the weather was damp and warm... ideal growing conditions for the ergot that grew on the wheat and rye which formed the peasants stable diet."

She paused.

"Ergot carries compounds related to the active ingredients of psychoactive drugs like LSD. Those peasants were out of their minds, seeing and believing things which were not happening. You and your chums spent the better part of an evening inhaling the spores of a mutated strain of fungus which drives people insane."

And there it was. The explanation, in black and white starkly stated terms.

An experiment in boosting cereal crop yields that had gone horribly wrong.

"Everyone has an inner life, their particular interests and obsessions," the visitor continued. "Your chums each had unconscious desires that became the focus of their mania, enclosed feedback loops, self-fulfilling prophecies, echo chambers... vicious circles. There is an ancient symbol for eternity in the form of a snake devouring its own tail; that's what happened to your friends. Their minds ate themselves."

"Because they inhaled fungal spores?" Robin asked quietly.

"Yes; the wheat had passed genes selected for hardiness onto the ergot, and the ergot survived in their systems, in their lungs, releasing more and more psychoactive toxins into them..."

"But what about me? If any of what your saying is true, shouldn't the same have happened to me? Shouldn't I have gone crazy?"

She smiled.

"Can't you guess? Your... treatment," she said. "Or at least, that's the boffin's theory, all to do with hormone levels and what not. Quid pro quo, tell me about the circle you made."

Robin sat back in the bed and chewed upon a bottom lip.

I have no choice, do I? She's answered so many questions, but there was this last one; why me? Why haven't I lost my mind like the rest, and committed an atrocity?

A pause.

The visitor was watching. Robin wouldn't meet those mirthless eyes.

Instead, looking at the sunflowers in the jar at the side of the, tracing the concentric patterns of the seeds that ran around and around in a tightening spiral, the story continued where it had been left.

THE CIRCLE
Part Three

FOUR weaving and bobbing lights descended the sloping bank at just after midnight. Two of them were singing, and occasionally a third would join in. The fourth was overweight and stuffed full of sausage meat and bread and beer, and was too out of breath to sing along, even though he knew the words as well as the others.

> *"A mother was washing*
> *Her baby one night,*
> *The youngest of ten*
> *And a delicate mite..."*

It was their anthem, as stupid as it was.

> *"The mother turned round*
> *For a soap off the rack,*
> *She was only a moment,*
> *But when she turned back..."*

The boys could barely keep a tune, but they didn't need to. The delivery was done in the broadest, most ludicrously over-the-top Cockney accents they could muster.

"Her baby was gone..."

This came out as; 'er babby woz gornn...

"And in anguish she cried,
'Oh where has my baby gone?'
The angel's replied..."

Robin's dad collected LP's, originals for the most part, but he wasn't so precious about them that he wouldn't let his son play them; he was hoping a taste for "good music, proper music" would rub off on him. This hope was all but dashed when the boys had turned thirteen and Fat Andy decided they should form an extreme black metal band called Korpsefukka.

"Oh!
Your!
Baby has gone down the plughole!"

Robin had only put Cream's *Disraeli Gears* on the turntable because he liked the psychedelic cover art. It was alright, overall, he conceded, lying on his bed and leisurely masturbating on that Thursday evening years ago, thinking about his crush... and then the final track played, a song that was completely like any of the bluesy psychedelic rock that had come before it, called "Mother's Lament."

He hadn't finished the wank. He'd listened to the track five times in a row instead, and then invited the boys over with a huge grin on his face.

"Oh your baby has gone down the plug!"

Oh yer babby 'as gornn dahn da plug!
It was the funniest thing any of them had heard, a bizarre old song from the East End about a mum washing her baby in the ink, only for the infant to get flushed down the plughole. They'd learned the words by heart, and whenever they got drunk it always came out, and every time they sang it there Cockney accents became ever more exaggerated.

"The poor little thing was so very thin,
He should have been washed in a jug!"

Then, crooning;

"In a juuuugggg!"

They didn't get to finish the song, the final reassurance from the angels that the baby was in Heaven and wouldn't need a bath anymore, because they had come to the field.

"Right," said Robin, slapping his hands together in the dark. "Let's do this fucking thing!"

Dildo and Shades shouted their assent. Fat Andy belched, which was as good as.

Robin marvelled; he felt amazing, better than he had in... well, it wasn't forever, but it almost felt like it. Being told you only so many months left trapped in your body had a weird effect on your perception of time. And right now he felt amazing. The booze would be part of it, of course, and the camaraderie, yes. Was adrenaline a part of it? Yes, that too, but there was something else, something more fundamental; he hadn't felt like this since he was young, a teenager, with the future before him. This was just like the stupid shit they used to do together on wild nights, a stupid scheme, a crazed lark, with no logic behind it but just having a laugh and knowing or caring nothing about consequences.

An adventure.

And in the glow of the headlamps they each wore, they were young again.

*****

Making crop circles requires very little in the way of equipment, mainly rope and planks of wood. A circle is easily drawn by holding a rope at one end, playing out half the length needed for the projected circles diameter, and then walking around in a circle. The wood is used to flatten broad patches of the crop down, moving in one direction to create the swirling pattern.

The planks had been sourced by Shades; kitchen supplies to the prison where he worked tended to be on an industrial scale and came in on wooden pallets. A few broken ones had been left behind the loading bay, and with the blessing of the supplies manager he had ripped a few planks free to take home with him.

Robin had bought a few reels of blue nylon rope from B&Q, and a few other bits and pieces, such as the headlamps.

The design was simple, classical. Two large circles side by side for the balls, a smaller circle ten yards away for the tip of the cock, and then straight parallel lines connecting the tip to the balls with a long, thick shaft. Then, when the basic outline was done, they could add fine details, such as a few squiggly lines for pubes on the balls, and some tear drop shapes shooting out of the tip to represent a nice big ejaculation.

They had practiced in Fat Andy's back garden until they were pretty confident in each of their roles, but the reality of the situation was a bit different as they were now, a) reliant on only their personal illumination rather than the full sunlight they had been enjoying in the garden, b) trying to push down a growing crop that was already shoulder height rather than the overgrown lawn which Fat Andy had neglected for a few weeks, and c) hadn't practiced with a skin full of cheap lager.

As they worked they chatted, a constant stream of banter, the kind of free-flowing conversation that only old friends can manage.

Towards the end, a debate broke out amongst them whether or not the cock should be ejaculating. The sides were evenly weighted, with both Andy and Robin arguing that it was the artistic piece of flair that was needed, whilst their fellow circle conspirators held to the opinion that they should not, as most graffiti cocks you saw did not have streamers of melted ice-cream shooting from the end.

This description of male ejaculate provoked such laughter, however, that the argument was clinched by the side that had actually opposed it, and the four of them spent their last twenty minutes creating the effect in trodden grass whilst swapping increasingly wild euphemisms for the substance they were depicting.

"People porridge!"

"Man muck!"

"Filthy concrete!"

"Malenanaise!"

"You what?"

"It's a portmanteau of male and mayonnaise."

"Ooo, look at the writer with his fancy technical terms! Portmanteau my Aunt fucking Fanny."

"Then you do better, lard-lad."

"Fuck you, alright; dick snot, cock hock, happy spaff, hate paste!"

Drunken laughter under a starry summer sky.

When they were done they took it in turns to Christen their creation. One by one, they walked into the middle of the biggest circle, took out their cocks, and turned clockwise, pissing golden streams. And of course, each was in turn abused by his fellows;

"Fat Andy's got his saveloy out! No, hang about, that's a fucking chipolata!"

"Hey Dildo, that looks like a cock… only smaller!"

"Here Shades, do you know what the German word for "virgin" is, 'cos it looks like you need to know! Do ya? Schneisseundtight!"

"Jeepers Creepers, Jewboy, did your parents not tell the Rabbi when to stop cutting?"

Each of them was coughing as they returned to their camp, the chaff and dust they had raised up during their night's work clinging about them, getting into their clothes and hair and lungs. Happy and exhausted, they each lay down and slept, out on the bare hillside, tents forgotten, sleeping bags used as mattresses, until dawn crept over the trees to the East.

They rose, moaning about hangovers, declaring that they'd never drink again and whose fucking clever idea was it to kip outside, my back is fucked… but all complaints tapered off and were forgotten as their eyes turned down the slope to the field where they had been busy only hours before.

"Fuck me," said Fat Andy.

"Not even with Jewboy's cock," said Dildo.

"We did it," said Shades, and laughed. "Fucking hell, we did it lads, we really did it!"

It was a little wonky, but most dicks were, weren't they? Fifty yards long, veiny, with a stylised fountain of fish yogurt half that length again blowing from the tip and balls large enough to park a half dozen cars within, the pictogram dominated the field, made all the more impressive because the scarecrow with the shiny eyes was close by and provided a sense of true scale.

They mugged for selfies with the thing visible over their shoulders, laughing and laughing and proclaiming how fucking brilliant it was, how fucking amazing they were.

Fat Andy wrapped a meaty arm around Robin's thin shoulders and squeezed him hard.

"That," he said, pointing with his free hand at the crop circle, "what would you call that, Jewboy? Just what would you say that was?"

Robin smiled.

Fuck. He was crying.

But he got the words out;

"That, you tubby sack of shit, is a fuck-off massive cock with a pair of fuck-off massive fucking bollocks!"

They cheered, and that was it, that was the best day of the end of his life.

"THAT'S IT. The whole adventure. After that we went our separate ways, agreeing to get together again as soon as commitments allowed and... and we didn't, because my friends went crazy. The end."

At some point Robin had started crying. The tears had flowed freely, but the voice telling the story had remained strong. Mind's eye turned to memories, wishing they would last. Two palms rubbed sight clear to find the gaze had been staring at the sunflowers in the jar next to this bed the entire time, hypnotized.

Robin frowned. There was something wrong with the flowers.

"Cereal crops are the root of civilisation," said the visitor.

Startled from reverie and the odd puzzle of the sunflowers -something was off- Robin turned back to her.

"We were hunter gatherers, reliant on nature to provide," she said. "Small clans of Homo Sapiens moving with the seasons from one patch of earth to the next, collecting berries and roots where we could, supplementing our diet with whatever furry things we could catch. Then we recognised mother nature for the fickle whore she is and made her our slave. We took wild grasses and we cleared the land and planted crops, and that was the start.

By having control of the food supply we could provide for a larger clan. A larger clan needed set guidelines, rules. Laws. We created a way of controlling ever larger clans and called it society. We turned from having just enough to survive, to having an excess; this excess we learned to convert into beer and wine, and these too were useful for control."

Robin stared at her.

Her head titled slightly to one side.

"In the 18th century, a brewer called Arthur Guinness found a large amount of the barley he used in his craft horribly burnt in a storehouse fire. But do you know what he did? He turned a disaster into a success and created the drink we call Guinness from that scorched crop."

"Why are you telling me this?" Robin asked.

"You'll understand soon enough," she told him. "And now, I believe I owe you one more piece of history. Whatever happened to your dear chum Shades?"

SHADES
Nice & Tight

THE GREAT philosopher Fat Andy had once explained to his childhood chums that the disparity of how promiscuity was culturally observed between the genders was simple; "A bloke who fucks a lot is a stud and a bird who fucks a lot is a slag for a fucking good reason; a key that opens a lot of locks is a master key… but a lock opened by many keys is just a shitty fucking lock."

Shades knew about locks, and he wanted to argue, but he was never so good with words.

Locks work both ways.

In a prison, they are there to keep the inmates in.

But they can also be used to keep everyone else out.

HMP Winchester was on high-alert lock down even though no attempt had been made by any of its four hundred and eighty-two inmates to escape. The exact opposite in fact; a single member of staff had in fact triggered the lock down to stop anybody getting into Victoria Wing. He'd done so early in the morning, just after the shift change, so as to give himself the maximum amount of time before his colleagues would begin the process of breaking in to stop him.

Locks were jammed.

Electronic systems were disabled.

The CCTV cameras were all blind.

(*schneisseundtight*)

Blake Butcher, known to his childhood friends as Shades, was doing the Lord's work, and did not wish to be disturbed.

*****

Each of the men who came around to find themselves restrained had similar muddled thoughts. Most of them wondered at first why they hurt so much; their muscles ached as if they had run a marathon carrying a rucksack of bricks, and their heads throbbed in that way that makes a person swear off booze for the rest of their lives.

After this inventory of pain was complete, memory would kick in and try to explain why they felt this way. Memory would remind them that they were caged men, doing time, stir, porridge... that they were prisoners of Her Majesty's Pleasure, and that their physical condition could therefore have nothing to do with running marathons or epic drinking sessions.

Attempting to resolve this seeming paradox, their brain's would supply each of them with a similar scenario recently lodged in the short-term section of their memory, to whit, the last thing they could recall; the door of their cell opening, and a member of staff entering, holding something in his right hand which suddenly jumped and whipped towards them and then... nothing.

Most of the men had never been hit with a taser before, and so had no frame of reference for puzzling out the connection between this final recollection and their returning to a state of pained, and restrained, consciousness.

Only one of them could have figured this out, having been rendered unconscious by taser several times in his life -as well as by administered drugs, choke-holds, and by plain old fashioned beatings- but this gentleman, a man legally known as Irvine Campbell and by the national press as the Monster of Easterhouse, wasn't interested in the "how" or even the "why", so much as "what the fuck?"

He, along with three other men from the wing, were stood around a pool table.

Well, stood in a technical sense. He was supported somehow, his back lashed to something, his arms as well, stuck out at right angles like he was crucified... exactly like he was crucified, in fact, if the three other men all shared the same situation as him. Naked, arms akimbo, stood at the corners of the table with their genitals dangling in the holes.

Irvine tried to move. This was when he discovered his legs were fixed to the table with superglue, his thighs pressed firmly against the wood.

The pool tables were the large, heavy kind you found in pubs, the kind which retained the balls after potting, requiring the deposit of more money to play another frame. There were three of them on the landing between the cells, for use during the single hour of free association afforded to the inmates every afternoon.

Irvine tried to make a comment on the situation that would have expressed his bemusement, couched in terms of extreme profanity and roared at the top of his Glaswegian accent, but found his mouth was taped shut.

Just like the others.

Being a predator, even if he was a caged predator, made the situation intolerable to Irvine. His head whipped back and forth as if in panic, but he was in fact taking everything in, absorbing information to be processed and used.

To his left was Mitchel Mullen, that ginger cunt with the glass eye who'd knocked up his own daughter. To the right, at the opposite end of the table, with his usually neat black hair and moustache mussed from sleep, was SukkiBhati, who'd been a manager of one of those trampoline fun centres, a place he'd used to select the kids he'd stalk and attack on their journey's to school weeks afterwards. And diagonally opposite Irvine's position, with a huge pot belly and bald head, was Steven Queen.

The one who did the babies.

Irvine observed how the others were coming around as if rousing from bad dreams. Their lolling heads would roll and rise, eyes blinking open, and their bodies would twitch as they tried to move and found that they could not. Sounds of muffled confusion came next and wildly staring eyes full of confusion and fear.

"At the same time came the disciples unto Jesus, saying, Who is the greatest in the kingdom of heaven?"

Irvine placed the voice immediately; Mr Butcher, the Bible basher.

That eliminated a theory that had been bubbling in the back of his mind. Judging by the company he kept at the table, Irvine had the notion that prisoners from another wing had broken in and were going to torture them. There was a reason why Victoria Wing was extra secure; not just to keep the sex offenders banged up, but to stop the murderers and violent psychos that made up the rest of the prison's population -murderers and psychos who often had kids- from getting at those they considered pure scum.

But Blake wouldn't have had anything to do with such a scenario. The man was as clean as they came. He'd even had a few theological discussions with Irvine... in fact the last had been only a few days ago, about the parable of the tares, about what Jesus had meant by separating weeds from the harvested grain at the end of time.

So what the fuck was going on?

The officer appeared at Irvine's right. Irvine twisted his head to look at him, and tried asking his question even though he was still gagged.

Blake held a pool cue. He was chalking the end.

"And Jesus called a little child unto him, and set him in the midst of them, and said, Verily I say unto you, Except ye be converted, and become as little children, ye shall not enter into the kingdom of heaven. Whosoever therefore shall humble himself as this little child, the same is greatest in the kingdom of heaven."

Because of being naked and in pain and confused, Irvine hadn't considered the green surface below him. It was set up for a game, the red and yellow balls racked into a triangle with the 8-ball just off-centre in the middle of the pack.

Irvine was at the end with the D marked on the green felt, where the cue ball was placed ready.

(*has my baby gone*)

The prison officer was sweating heavily and he was grinning. The grin didn't extend to his eyes, which seemed dull, unnatural, and somehow empty. Irvine Campbell was not a man of great imagination, except where it came to the psychological manipulation of the boys who had trusted him, but he was put in mind of peeled hard boiled eggs onto which someone had drawn black spots with a permanent marker.

The pupils were so dilated there was almost no colour around them at all.

Butcher slapped the shaft of the pool cue against the palm of his hand. It made a slight *twang* noise. It was the dodgy one, the one whose tip didn't screw in very tight, the cue nobody ever played with.

Evidently, he had used all the good ones making the crucifixes that the sex offenders were lashed too.

"And whoso shall receive one such little child in my name receiveth me," said Butcher, his voice strong and rolling with righteousness. "But whoso shall offend one of these little ones which believe in me, it were better for him that a millstone were hanged about his neck, and that he were drowned in the depth of the sea. Woe unto the world because of offences! for it must needs be that offences come; but woe to that man by whom the offence cometh!"

The prison officer bent at the waist and lined up his shot.

He made the break.

The neat triangle of balls broke apart almost languidly, the sudden impact of the cue ball striking them with a loud *crack* belying how they shock of the impact spread evenly throughout the crowd. Reds and yellows split, like a demonstration of the nucleus of an atom coming apart, rolling to rest in a pattern as meaningless as stars in the night sky.

The cue ball rolled to a stop halfway down the table.

Officer Butcher strode around to it, eyes assessing the table, picking out possibilities.

A red ball was covering the pocket inches from where SukkiBhati's genitals dangled, his brown cock and balls furred by grey pubic hair. His testicles hung heavy in the hole, like a leather punching bag in a boxing gym.

A straight shot. Easy.

Butcher smashed the cue ball as hard as he could. It pounded into the red with a loud *crack* and the red punched hard into Sukki's dangling testicles.

He screamed behind his duct tape, his whole body quivering with pain as his eyes flared wide open.

Irvine winced in sympathy, and felt his own bollocks threatening to retreat up into his abdomen.

The red ball didn't have enough room to fall into the pocket, and had become wedged in the gap, the child molester's genitals trapping it in place.

Butcher reached over with the tip of his cue, holding it with one hand, and tapped on the top of the ball, forcing it down the gap.

The vibration of the ball being forced against testicles that had almost burst was enough to make Sukki vomit, but having nowhere to go, the sick flooded his sealed mouth and spewed out of his nostrils in twin streams of yellow bile.

The sound of the potted ball rolling through the table's insides underlined the spluttering and snorting of the man with the crushed testicles.

(*oh! your!*)

Sukki was struggling to breathe with his sinuses full of puke.

Butcher was lining up another shot. For the same pocket.

As he leant over to line himself up, he quoted the next part of a bible passage which had been running through his head for a fortnight on and off and continuously for the past twenty-four hours, non-stop, over and over, mixed up with an old song from happier days;

"Wherefore if thy hand or thy foot offend thee, cut them off, and cast them from thee; it is better for thee to enter into life halt or maimed, rather than having two hands or two feet to be cast into everlasting fire."

A hard slap shot that smashed another ball into the already bruised and bleeding testes.

(*baby has gone the plughole!*)

Sukki howled behind his gag, his head thrashing wildly, streamers of snot and sick whipping left and right.

Butcher straightened up. The sweat was flowing steadily down his face now, great drops rolling down his forehead and cheeks, and even over the lips of his wide and fixed grin.

"Hate the sin, not the sinner," he said. "I believe in forgiveness. I believe in rehabilitation. I believe none are so fallen from grace that they cannot find their way back to the Father if they are truly repentant. Hate the sin, not the sinner. Sukki, are you sorry for what you did? All those innocent ones you corrupted?"

Sukki didn't seem to be hearing him. He was sobbing and snuffling, tears rolling down to join the snot and vomit that was rolling over the duct tape that bound his mouth.

Officer Butcher moved out of Irvine's line of sight.

When he reappeared, he walked up behind Sukki.

He reached around the man's torso with one hand and grasped his cock. He pulled it straight up, stretching it over the saggy flesh of the child molesters' stomach.

"My mate Andy used to do this all the time," said Butcher. "He'd pull his dick out and do this and he'd say, hey, look, I bought the last chicken in Tesco! And it really does look like a chicken, doesn't it?"

Sukki's eyes were round, wide open so that white could be seen right around his irises.

Butcher's other hand snaked around the other side of Sukki's waist.

The officer had evidently raided the kitchen for supplies.

"Hate the sin, not the sinner," he said.

The electric carving knife had two serrated blades aligned next to each other, barely two millimetres separating them so that they were almost a single cutting edge. Butcher eased them under Sukki's abused testicles, hefting the bruised bag on them and making the man wince and squeal.

"And if thine eye offend thee, pluck it out, and cast it from thee," said the insane prison officer. "It is better for thee to enter into life with one eye, rather than having two eyes to be cast into hell fire."

His thumb pushed the *ON* button.

The blades buzzed into life, sliding back and forth faster than the eye could see with a high pitched whirring sound... a sound that was soon joined by Sukki's muffled screams as the electric knife cut into his scrotal sack as easy as if they were cutting into the breast meat of an uncooked chicken, fresh from the slaughter.

Shredded skin and pubes and bright blood flew from the man's crotch, splattering his thighs and belly and appearing as brown, comet shaped stains across the green baize of the pool table.

Irvine didn't want to see what happened, but he couldn't stop himself. His eyes wouldn't close, his brain wouldn't let him close out the horror.

The electric carving knife chewed up through Sukki's genitals, sounding angry at having to rip through thick skin and gristle rather than moist cooked meat. Officer Butcher earned his name as he kept his grip on the man's cock, still pulling it upwards, until finally penis and testicles ripped away from Sukki's crotch in a welter of hot blood and agony.

At some point the man had passed out from pain or shock or both, his head lolling forward, snot and tears and sick dripping to mix with the pulsing blood flowing from the raw wound where his genitals had been, into the pocket of the pool table.

Butcher put the carving knife down on the side of the table, reached up, gripped one edge of the duct tape over Sukki's mouth, and ripped it off. Dammed puke instantly flooded out over his lips and chin, but the pervert didn't come around.

Not even when the prison officer pushed the bloody mass of his sexual organs into his mouth, making his cheeks bulge.

As Butcher fed Sukki his own cock and balls, he recited the last part of the bible passage that was stuck in his head, in a grotesque parody of the act of communion;

"Take heed that ye despise not one of these little ones; for I say unto you, That in heaven their angels do always behold the face of my Father which is in heaven."

When he was done, he wiped his bloody hands on his uniform trousers and turned his grin back to the three remaining men.

"Right then," he said through his grin. "Who wants to see a trick shot?"

*****

Outside the wing, Blake "Shades" Butcher's colleagues were still working on trying to get in.

Prisoners in the other wings were still in their cells. The decision to keep everyone locked up was an obvious one, seeing as though no-one knew exactly what was going on, but this disruption to the everyday grinding rituals of prison life was always dangerous. HMP Winchester housed some of the country's most violent men, men who had hair-triggers on their tempers, men who did not care about reason. Any grievance or slight was amplified in the mind of the average inmate tenfold, and their responses were always completely out of all proportion.

And quite a number of the men in Albert Wing had been working on a long-term project.

The prison was a century and a half old, and thanks to nearly a generation of cuts to public services, in poor repair. Mortar which was once as solid as the bricks it held in place had become crumbly in critical spaces, age decayed, such as around the frames of cell doors. This information was widely known amongst the population, and certain members had been working agonisingly slowly on teasing out more and more of the decaying building material. This material was flushed down the toilet or thrown out of the tiny slits in the windows that acted as ventilation.

In some cells, entire bricks could even be removed.

Few of the inmates involved in this gradual dismantling had any real reason to believe that their actions would lead to something like a jail break - that was all in films, a load of bollocks- but they did have a nose for mischief. Remove enough bricks quickly enough and a slender man could squeeze out... and if only a handful of them were able to make it to the landing, then who knew what possibilities for devilry could be had?

Particularly on a morning when something was obviously afoot elsewhere in the prison... something that was distracting the staff... and causing the bored but well-rested men of Albert Wing to miss their fucking breakfast...

*****

When the third yellow ball smashed into Mitchel Mullen's testicles he came back to consciousness again and wished he was dead.

Like many of the sex offenders on Victoria Wing, Mitchel was not a hardened criminal. He had, in fact, lead a rather soft and easy life, and it was only when his fourteen year old daughter's baby was born with a crown of curly red hair and deep blue eyes that were an echo of his that Mitchel's world unravelled.

Her condition wasn't obvious until it wasn't too late for a termination and so he had told her to lie about what had happened. He had told her to say she was raped walking home from school five months previously, and that she had not wanted to say anything because she had felt so dirty and ashamed. Mitchell had coached his daughter well and reinforced his will upon her by using all the psychological manipulation that he had perfected over four years of secretly fucking her.

Unfortunately, she had embellished the story of the rape with her own creative twist and had quietly told her mother that it was a *black* man who had done it.

Genetics can be a roll of the dice. The newborn had no hint of heritage beyond the Celtic, though that did not necessarily mean the father couldn't have been black. But Raquel Mullen had taken one look at her first grandchild and in a devastating instance of psychic overload had known everything.

Mitchel's first experience of real pain had been when his screeching wife had attacked him in the hospital waiting room.

The quick action of the maternity nursing staff had managed to save one of his eyes.

The agony of the first two strikes to his balls had made him pass out. The third was enough to burst his left testicle and attained such heights of lunatic pain that it brought him back to full wakefulness.

"Then were there brought unto him little children, that he should put his hands on them, and pray; and the disciples rebuked them."

Irvine Campbell noted in a distracted way that prison officer Blake Butcher had moved from Matthew 18:1-10 to Matthew 19:13-15.

The cue was laid down and the electric carving knife was picked up again.

He stood behind Mitchel and reached around, but this time he did not drag the man's penis up over his stomach as he had done with Sukki. Instead, he made a fist around it and began to pump it back and forth.

Irvine couldn't believe what he was seeing. Of course, everything he had seen so far was unbelievable, but this was something else; Butcher was wanking Mitchel.

"But Jesus said, Suffer little children to come unto me," said the prison office, almost into the ear of the man whose cock he was squeezing and groping, like they were words of endearment, "for of such is the kingdom of heaven."

And somehow, Mitchel's body was responding. Thickening.Lengthening.

Soon, Butcher had a lazy semi in the palm of his hand.

He stopped pumping it, gripping the pasty white thing by the root. It still had a considerable amount of foreskin covering the hood, the ruffles of skin looking like some kind of bizarre fleshy rose flower.

"I have a Jewish friend," said Butcher conversationally. "Though I don't hold it against him as he isn't very observant. He told me a good joke once." Butcher's grin seemed to widen by a fraction of an inch, and the sweat continued to ooze down his face. "What happened to the blind man who got a job doing circumcisions?"

He thumbed the electric carving knife's *ON* switch. The blades buzzed to life, and tiny fragments of Sukki's genetic material flicked away from them.

"He got the sack!"

Butcher brought the whirring blades down half an inch from the end of Mitchel's still semi-hard penis.

Behind his gag of duct tape, Mitchel screamed, and even as muffled as it was, Irvine felt his back and arms ripple with goose flesh at the sound. No person should ever have uttered a sound like that, a cry of such wordless pain and utter despair.

The glans of Mitchel's cock plopped onto the green baize of the pool table, still hooded in the wrinkles of foreskin.

Blood squirted in time to the man's heartbeat, scarlet ejaculations from the ragged stump of raw meat fringed by shredded skin.

Butcher lifted the still whirring blades, moved them back along the shaft another half an inch, and sliced down again.

An absurd memory suddenly flashed in Irvine's mind; his childhood, back home in Glasgow, a fish supper from the chippy, only he never had cod or hake, he always had a saveloy sausage and his mam would cut it up for him into neat little chunks with a steak knife...

Nausea washed through him. His stomach seemed to coil in on itself, like a snail retreating tightly into its shell.

The next segment of severed cock rolled on the lip of the pocket, then fell in.

Mitchel's eyes had gone back in his head and his whole body was jerking with convulsions, threatening to break the cross of cues he was lashed to.

The blade came down again, but the result was far messier; the blood that had plumped Mitchel's dick was now a spreading puddle on the table, leaving the length of organ in Butcher's fist a soft mass that got caught between the rapidly sliding blades, spraying flecks of skin and tiny cobs of erectile tissue left and right.

Mitchel choked to death on his tongue before Butcher was finished with him, slicing off his balls with a careless stroke that left a huge gash on the man's inner thigh.

"And he laid his hands on them, and departed thence," finished the prison officer, his eyes cast down.

When he looked back up, his gaze locked with Irvine's.

*****

Blake Butcher's fellow prison officers were pretty close to undoing the damage he had done to the various safety measures on the wing's security -

he had both literally snapped keys in locks, and had done so figuratively on the computer systems- when the riot broke out on Albert Wing.

This bought Butcher the time he needed to finish the Lord's work.

*****

"I have a pet theory about you, Mr Queen," said prison officer Butcher.

And then, as an afterthought, sweat sliding down his face as if he were stood under a dribbling tap, he said, "Baby has gone."

For his part, Steven Queen had his eyes clamped tightly shut and his flesh was shuddering as fear coursed through his veins like ice water. The mention of his surname made his eyes pop open briefly, eyes the startling blue of sapphires, but when he caught sight of what Butcher was holding he immediately snapped them shut again and started making noises that were muffled and impossible to assign to words, but whose meaning was otherwise abundantly clear; he was pleading for his life, asking for mercy.

The electric carving knife wasn't the only item Butcher had retrieved from the prison's kitchen.

"An awful lot of time and money has been done into researching paedophilia," said Butcher, truly looking like his name sake now with the meat cleaver in his right hand. He was walking around the table, around and around, circling behind Irvine's back and then behind Steven's, the great blade in his hand swaying back and forth as he spoke. "I've read the studies published in the journals, and I like to think I have a firm grasp of the various theories, nature versus nurture and all that, learned behaviour the result of childhood abuse, or a genetic component... And whilst I'll admit my theory is crude and not backed up by a great deal of data, I do believe that it is informed by a number of years of experience working amongst the resident population of kiddy fiddlers."

Butcher stopped walking. He was stood just behind Irvine, who felt his flesh cold-crawl with anticipation.

"You want to be big," said Butcher in a reasonable tone.

(*schneisseundtight*)

Irvine awaited the moment that the hand would come for him, snaking around his waist to grasp the glands that made him a male... but Butcher walked on.

"That's it," he said. "That's all. You've got a tiny willy, so small that even if you can find a grown woman to stick it into, she's going to spend the entire time asking you if you're in yet. But what can you do? Almost nothing! So, according to my friend Dildo who almost became a doctor, all those adverts in your email inbox for pills to make your todger grow are all utter bollocks. And there's no surgery that can make you bigger; as Dildo pointed out to me once, if there were a pill or an operation to make dick's bigger, whoever invented it would be a bloody billionaire, and we'd all know their name!"

He stopped behind Steven. Steven shivered even more, and if it were possible, his eyes screwed even more tightly shut.

"Maybe my theory is a bit simplistic, but, see, as a modern Christian who eschews the notion of supernatural evil... as a modern Christian who believes in the goodness of God's creation, and that no man is beyond the reach of His loving forgiveness... I have to believe such a crude, simplistic, idiotic notion, because the alternative is so much worse... That men can truly be that evil, and God has abandoned us."

Irvine saw the man shrug. He held the meat cleaver up and admired its keen edge; the blade was a foot long and at least eight inches wide.

"But I've got a solution. In fact, Mr Queen, you lucky fellow, I've done Dildo proud and come up with a surgical procedure which will leave you with a dick that can *touch the ground!*"

Butcher gripped the handle of the meat cleaver with both hands and swung it like a lumberjack swinging an axe to fell a tree. The heavy blade chopped into the top of Steven's thigh just below his hip, with a thick, meaty sound, like someone with solid abdominal muscles taking a punch in the gut.

Steven screamed into the duct tape that covered his mouth.

Above this noise, Butcher's voice rose strong as he quoted scripture;

"Another parable put he forth unto them, saying, The kingdom of heaven is likened unto a man which sowed good seed in his field; But while men slept, his enemy came and sowed weeds among the wheat, and went away."

The prison officer pulled the cleaver free. Three quarters of the blade's width was sunk into the pervert's flabby flesh, and it slid out with a gush of blood.

The wound gaped like a toothless grin, idiotic and full of glistening red muscle.

"But when the blade was sprung up, and brought forth fruit, then the weeds appeared also."

Butcher swung the blade again.

This time as the blade hacked into bone, the sound it made was actually like what you'd expect to hear if it were an axe chopping into a tree.

Steven screamed again, higher and harder than before, a tea kettle rising to the boil, though the sound was muffled as if the kettle were wrapped in heavy fabric.

Butcher had a harder job pulling the cleaver out this time, as it had chopped most of the way into the screaming man's thigh bone. With the blood that was flowing freely from the wound slicking the blade and running down the handle, he had to tightly wrap both hands around it and then, bracing his foot against the side of the pool table, pushed with his foot and pulled with his hands, wiggling the blade back and forth before it came free with a moist little squeak.

"So the servants of the householder came and said unto him, Sir, didn't you sow good seed in thy field?" said the prison officer. "From where did the weeds come out from?"

He swung for a third time.

The blade hacked through the remaining bone and passed out through the flesh of Steven's inner right thigh, and bit into the inside of his left.

The man's entire leg was severed, but he was held in place by the crucifix up his back and his other leg still glued to the table. Blood pulsed in a sick tide from the ragged wound, running down over his knee and coating his shin and calf like a glistening scarlet stocking.

"He said unto them, An enemy hath done this. The servants said unto him, Wilt thou then that we go and gather them up?"

Irvine watched with a hollowness inside him. There was nothing left; the past forty-two minutes -oh yes, only forty-two minutes, the clock high up on the wall that marked off the wasted hours of the inmates lives could tell no lies- had scooped him empty of all emotion, and left him only as a witness, a camera recording without judgement.

"But he said, Nay; lest while ye gather up the weeds, ye root up also the wheat with them." said Butcher, panting with exertion, still grinning, still sweating.

The prison officer flipped the blade over and readjusted his grip, then swung a heavy blow at Steven Queen's left leg.

This time the cleaver chopped through the thigh muscle and into the underlying bone on the first swing.

Breathing hard, Butcher pulled the blade free and lifted it even higher over his shoulder. His knuckles turned white as his gripped tightened and he readied himself for the hardest swing yet, a lumberjack about to deliver the final strike that would fell the tree... or a reaper about to make the final swing of the scythe that will bring in the harvest.

And he spoke;

"Let both grow together until the harvest: and in the time of harvest I will say to the reapers, Gather ye together first the weeds, and bind them in bundles to burn them: but gather the wheat into my barn!"

The second blow finished the job.

Steven Queen was legless, yet still perched on top of the legs that were glued to the table. His face was pure white, and his lips were purple, but somehow he was still alive, if barely conscious.

The prison officer nodded his approval.

"You see? Your dick will touch the ground now!"

He paused.

"Actually, maybe I should stick with the Lord's first plan like I did for Mr Mullen and Mr Bhati. Yes, probably best if I simply remove the temptation to fuck children entirely."

Blake Butcher reached around Steven's body like he was giving him a bear hug, but instead grabbed the child molester's genitals and severed them from his body with two long saw-like strokes of the cleaver.

Cock and balls in one hand, he used the red-dripping blade to cut through the duct tape that secured Steven's arms and torso to the improvised crucifix.

"...cast it from thee," said the prison officer, and chucked his bloody handful of glands and erectile tissue across the table.

They landed in front of Irvine, splattering to a rest against the table's rear cushion. They looked like a baby bird had fallen from the nest and been savaged by a cat.

Steven Queen saw his genitals tossed across the table and dimly realised that they were quite important.

He lifted one free arm and lent forward.

Like an Easter Island statue being desecrated, he toppled. Fountains of blood arced from the stumps of his thighs, yet somehow he stayed alive long enough to crawl across the table, tenderly collect his castrated manhood, and cuddle it to his chest before he died.

*****

It was another two hours before the situation in Albert Wing was brought under control and, finally, the staff of HMP Winchester were able to gain access to Victoria.

From the cells came a clamour of voices demanding to know what was going on, but it would be some time before the inmates would be attended to.

None of the staff could have been described as squeamish, but afterwards, two would resign, and another three asked for transfers to other prisons around the country.

The extreme mutilation performed on the four bodies was stomach churning enough.

But what was worse was what the survivor had to say.

Irvine Campbell had been a priest for twenty-two years, until one of his victims grew up and finally went to the police with the story of what the Father had done to him as an altar boy. Blake Butcher had chosen Irvine to be the one to hear his confession and receive his communion... the former holy man had vomited over and over again, but the prison officer had kept picking up the slivers and gobbets of his reproductive organs and forced them back into the man's mouth.

As Butcher had cut away his *own* cock and balls and forced Irvine to choke them down, he had spoken his confession, a confession jumbled up with chunks from the parable of the weeds and the wheat.

The police officers who broke into the Butcher flat later that day confirmed every detail of what the former priest had heard; Blake Butcher's wife was dead, and their unborn child had been removed from her womb.

They found Florence halfway round the u-bend of the flat's toilet.

The legal system being what it is, tests had to be run that no-one with any sense would have believed were necessary, confirming that the semen found in the foetus

(*has my baby gone*)

the semen found in her stomach

(*the angel's replied*)

and anus
(*oh! your!*)
and undeveloped vagina
(*baby has gone*)
was her father's.

IT WAS told, the final atrocity.

Robin felt utterly hollow. Numb.

"So now, so now, here we all, all up to date and filled in on

what's what," said the still nameless visitor. "Rather gruesome and grim business, all in all, hmm? I can finish my report on this nasty little incident ready for the bigwigs to decide what course of action is next, and you can... well, you have closure."

"This..." Robin said. "This can't be... how it ends."

In this simple expression was wound up a world of hurt. A life is said to pass before the eyes of the dying; childhood summers, the awkward and exhilarating nights of youth, the future always stretching before, such promise, such dreams... all shared with good friends with whom one strode forth into adulthood.

And it was all such a shit show in the end. You got older. Things didn't quite work out. You compromised. You told yourself it was okay. You kept busy, busy, busy, so you had no time to think.

You told yourself you were happy.

You went out with your mates and pretended everything was fine.

You denied who you fundamentally were because who you were didn't live in the world you lived in.

"Oh don't you worry, it's not," said the visitor. "Not just yet, anyway. You remember me telling you how Guinness is the result of a clever chap turning a disaster on its head?"

Robin looked at her as if she were the crazy one.

The visitor tried to look sympathetic. It was obviously an expression she hadn't had much practice with.

"So we created a monster," she said. "We created a strain of super-resistant, super-strong fungus that drives people to murderous insanity... that doesn't mean it can't be a nice little money spinner. Just imagine what would happen if a country's food supply could be used as a weapon. North Korea, for example, eat an awful lot of wheat noodles; supply some altered grain under the guise of international aid the next time they have a famine, wait for the first harvest, and watch the entire nation disembowel itself."

She shrugged.

"Biological warfare could be a new revenue stream for us, but we know you can't offer a poison for sale without proving it has an antidote. The boffins believe that it's your treatment that has been blocking the modified ergotamine in your system, stopping you turning into a lunatic. The R&D chaps want to know more. That's why we brought you here."

"Brought me here?" Robin asked. "What are you on about, I checked myself in weeks ago."

"You checked yourself into the hospital for the surgery. Then, yesterday, one of my colleagues administered a little something to your painkillers that put you out, and we transferred you here. This is one of our monitoring facilities."

Robin looked around the room.

Blandly cheerful, it certainly looked like a private room in...

The sunflowers in the jar next to the bed. The ones mum had brought in fresh just two days ago, cut from the corner of the garden which caught the full sun all day, perfect for growing record breakers.

Flowers that his mother had left as she fled weeping from the room, unable to pretend anymore.

A snatch of memory, some old cliché about weddings; don't think of it as losing a son, but gaining a daughter...

Robin reached over and touched their fake, plastic petals.

"Didn't you wonder how we found you?" asked her visitor. "From the moment you trespassed in our field we've been keeping an eye on you."

She didn't feel afraid. She'd been reborn, and that had taken all of her courage; to say goodbye to her friends rather than have them reject her, to even lose her mother, if it had to be.

And courage, used up, meant there was nothing for fear to be reflected in.

"How?" Robin asked.

"It's obvious you lot weren't country raised," she told him. "No farmer uses a bloody scarecrow anymore!"

The scarecrow on the far side of the field. Ripped jeans, gingham shirt, shiny eyes that caught the sunshine. He'd thought that was to make it look more life-like.

Camera lenses.

"We watched you, but what you did seemed harmless so we left you be. Then your friend Andy's face turned up in the papers and a colleague of mine recognised him. We don't believe in coincidences."

"Why didn't you stop them?"

The question seemed to surprise the visitor, though she did not ask Robin to clarify what she meant. She knew exactly what she meant; why didn't you stop them before they did what they did?

"Stop them? My dear little bird, you don't interfere with a running experiment, even if some random variables are introduced! Observation first, collation of results, then analysis. Which brings us full circle..."

Robin closed her eyes.

"...the boffins have all kinds of tests lined up..."

Like a snail, retreating deeper into the spiral of itself. Trying to blot out that voice.

"...blood work obviously, seeing as though you have the Y-chromsome, surgery and hormone injections can't change that..."

Maybe if she went deep enough she would find shelter, some place the pain wouldn't find her.

"...ultimately, yes, vivisection, I'm afraid."

The visitor paused.

The next question found Robin, deep down in the wound coil of the person she had always been inside.

"Which one of them was it?"

It was strange; when Robin had asked 'why didn't you stop them' this visitor hadn't asked for clarification. She'd known what was being asked.

And even though it seemed to lack context, Robin knew exactly what the question was.

And didn't answer.

"I know you never told your friends you were transitioning, that you preferred to tell them you were dying. Leave that life behind with a swift strike of the blade, like cutting off an unwanted... limb. I can make a good guess at the psychological reasoning behind your decision to never declare yourself. Understanding people is a large part of my work. I'm just asking out of curiosity, as I can't quite place my finger on which one you..."

"Andy," Robin said. She still didn't open her eyes. "It was always Andy. That's why I couldn't tell them, any of them. He was always the worst."

"Ah," said the visitor, nodding her head as if she saw exactly how this information slotted into the story. "I see it. Yes, of course it was. It had to be."

A pause.

"Love is a bastard, isn't it?"

She sighed and stood up.

"For what it's worth, my daughter is *a fan of your work."*

With one hand Robin gestured at the sketch she would never finish. The sketch which was supposed to be the end of her public confession.

"You can give her that. An original piece."

The woman took it.

"That is most kind of you! I don't suppose you would sign it, would you?"

Robin stared. Then, she picked up her sketching pencil and added her name, GINGER WASSER.

A nurse had come into the room, carrying a syringe.

The woman with the long grey hair took it, held it up to the light to check for bubbles.

"Okay, little bird," she said. "I'm afraid you might feel a little prick!"

She giggled, and as the male nurse held Robin still, slid the needle into her neck.

THE END

AUTHOR'S NOTE

I GREW up in the south of England, the home of crop circles. Every Summer in the school holidays, mum would take us out to see the latest designs, wonderful long hot days in which we and others would gather on the chalk hillsides to view the mysterious patterns that appeared in the wheat fields, before descending into those fields, after paying the farmer a quid or two, to wander and wonder. Were they the work of aliens? Were they the stigmata of the land? Or were they simply a drunken lark that got wildly out of hand?

As a teenager, I had two best mates. We did everything together, even though we were quite different; one of them was a kind of hippie/metal head who spoke as equally about karma as blast beats, and the other was the most embarrassing geek you could imagine, being loud and manic and constantly laughing his head off. The first time I got drunk was with them; the first time I tried drugs, with them. We did a lot of stupid shit and spent hours talking about everything and nothing. We even made a crop circle once, though it was a bit crude. Sometimes, in the Summer, we would go and make a fire in a clearing in the woods, and we'd sit around in a circle and dream aloud about what we would do when we were adults. The future was wide open and we were certain we were going to be special and make names for ourselves doing the things we loved.

My old mates.

They're both dead now.

One of them became a blacksmith. He loved working with his hands. He took a year out, and went to Bangkok where he bought a ratty old motorbike and rode all the way across South East Asia to the foothills of the Himalayas.

Not long after he came home he got killed by a drunk driver.

My other friend got a job in London, being paid a lot of money to do complicated mathematics in the City. He had one of those minds that can see how the universe fits together as a bunch of numbers and equations, and he could do his job whilst eating Thai green tofu curry in his flat overlooking the Thames.

He topped himself. Depression.

None of the characters in this story are us. I know that these four men are odious to a lot of people, representing various aspects of "toxic masculinity", but the friendship between them is the truth I wanted to write about, because that was our truth for as long as it lasted...

So here's to you, boys.

'Nother couple of dead soldiers.